The Ones

THE DARKEST SERIES

No place to hide
and no one to trust…

Jackie Mae

Cover design by, Carolyn Sheltraw
Edited by, Ashton Farmanara

Revised 2nd Edition

ISBN-13: 978-0-9916149-0-5 (paperback)/
         978-0-9916149-1-2 (ebook)

Printed in the United States of America

To Isabelle, who inspired me with her words

And to,

My husband—always my knight

Special Thanks To,

Haleh, Fary,
Rachel, and James
Your Support was Immense

A Note from Jackie Mae:

Welcome. Come along with me to a place where the Ones walk amongst us. Where ordinary people, like you and I, have hidden strengths. When all else fails, the meek shall not be mild, but bold and daring.

THE ONES (The Darkest Series) is the first book. A LIFETIME TO WAIT (The Darkest Series) is the next installment in the series.

I hope all my readers will enjoy the ride.

Contents

Chapter 1

The people started drifting away slowly. It was dinner time for most. There were still some people packing up, so she felt safe. She knew she should have brought Sammy, her beloved mixed breed, but the park was on her way home. Besides, Sammy had just been here yesterday. Next time. Next time she decided to leave early, and whenever she came back to the park in the future, she would bring her Sammy. Some people would call him Heinz 57, but not her. It wasn't majestic enough.

She lost track of time as she thought of memories gone by and things she should have accomplished by now. Slowly, she became aware that no one was left there except her. She knew she should have packed up and headed home to feed Sammy, but her thoughts wandered a few minutes more. Then she felt a push, ever so slight. It felt like a breeze rushing by to wrap her in its arms, to keep her safe. She felt a presence moving toward her. A malevolent presence—which wanted her. But how could she know that? The time for figuring things out was not now; definitely not now. She felt the push again. Time to go.

Somehow, she knew in all of her being that he was here. She knew not who he was, only that he was here. Anxious, nervous, and scared, she began walking swiftly, then running, toward her Honda. She felt a breeze upon her back raising the hair on her arms and neck. She was scared, definitely scared now, and there was no one around to call for help. Slowly, she turned to look around to only see that the once tranquil looking park now seemed somehow tainted and ominous. There was a power that she felt in her bones, so absolute that it was almost tangible. Should she leave the trail and head for the highway not more than a tenth of a mile to her left over some small rocks and an incline? Perhaps she could make it to the car. Wasting no time, she flat out ran toward her car.

"I love myself, I love myself," she mumbled. "Yes," she thought, as she hopped in her car and locked the doors. It was all in her imagination. She didn't see or hear anyone. *How silly of me, ridiculous actually.* She pulled out of the parking lot and lectured herself for being so scared. Although she had convinced herself on a reasonable level nothing had happened, that there was not even one tangible piece of evidence that anyone had been there, her purely emotional side disagreed.

She settled in for the trip back and turned on the radio to listen to the traffic and weather report. The tall picturesque trees, gently swaying in the breeze along the drive home, helped to settle her nerves. Everything seemed as it should be. Yet she had this nagging feeling, in every fiber of her being, that something monumental had just taken place.

In town, Claire decided to first stop at Ben's coffee shop to have a cup of java and be amongst her friends for a few minutes. The coffee and desserts were great and she knew some of her friends were bound to be there as well. It was just after dusk and people were starting to venture out after work. She would feel safe. Her friends would be there to talk some sense into her. As she walked in, she looked around until she saw Troy and Isabella, sitting by the window drinking coffee.

"Hey, how are you?" Isabella called from across the way.

"Just fine, just fine," replied Claire. That was her standard answer for family and friends. But she thought she would amend it this time. "Actually, I had this really strange and scary incident over at the park just now, but I'm sure it was just my imagination."

"Explain what happened," said Troy.

"Well, I went over to the park from work. I left early you see, and I stayed until dusk. I started getting this feeling that someone was watching me and it gave me the heebie-jeebies. I started walking toward my car. The whole time I was thinking about why I didn't stop by the condo and pickup Sammy, when the hair on the back of my neck told me to hurry. It really scared me guys. I'm so silly. It was nothing, nothing at all. I ran like a girl to my car, locked the doors, and looked around. There wasn't anyone in sight."

Troy and Isabella assured her it must have been stress, due to the work load she had been carrying this month at work.

Isabella leaned forward with her fingers steepled together as if in deep concentration. "Claire, you know you have been working late hours and weekends since the pilot program began last year. I am so happy you finally took the afternoon off, but this issue of feeling that someone was following you disturbs me."

"Me too," Troy added. "Listen, you should take a couple of days off. Say, you could go to Seattle and stay with my sister, Lizzie, no problem. She's a teacher as you know, and loves to see you."

"I know Troy, but I can't just call in and take off."

"Why not? I mean, it's not like the place would fall apart for a few days. You must have oodles of vacation time piling up. You need this Claire, you know you do," responded Troy.

"I'll think about it." *But not too seriously.*

Isabella and Troy glared at her saying nothing. They were right. She needed to get her head straight. She couldn't go around searching the shadows for someone lurking about waiting for her. It sounded ridiculous. If someone had told her the same story she would be headed in the other direction after suggesting a good doctor.

"Ok, I'll do it," she said impulsively. "Are you sure Lizzie wouldn't mind? I can call my boss tonight and explain I really need a few days off to see an old friend."

"Sure thing, no problem" said Troy. "I'll call Lizzie right now, Claire. We love you, you know. Isabella and I are grateful for everything you've done for us."

"Yes, I know. I love you guys right back." She hadn't done much. Not really. She met Isabella and Troy at a convention six years ago and attended a few workshops with them. They went out to lunch a few times and she knew instantly she liked them.

They were so happy, friendly, and always concerned for others. She stayed in touch and when she had heard that they had lost their house in a short-sale, due to job loss, she had simply called her friend, Jake Summers. Jake owed her a favor or two. She'd asked if he could possibly help Troy in any way. Jake was so impressed with Troy that he was hired on at his firm with an increase in pay no less, and they had managed to straighten out their credit and repurchase a home just this year.

Troy went off to call Lizzie, and Isabella took the opportunity to talk privately with her. "Tell me the truth, was someone following you?"

"I felt someone breathing on my neck, and the hair on the back of my neck stood up. It took me a few seconds to gather the courage to stop and look behind me, but I did. No one was there that I could see, but I felt someone close by. I can't explain it any better. It was like nothing I have ever felt before. It really scared me. At first, I had this dreamy feeling of a lover I needed to be with, and then I woke up to reality and got scared. I am a practical girl, Isabella; I don't fantasize about lovers or scary shadows following me. That's not like me at all."

"Claire, this really disturbs me; you know you feel things others do not."

"My God, don't talk so loud." She looked around anxiously. She spoke softly, "I don't want Troy, or anyone else to know that. Do not mention it around Troy, Isabella. You, and God as my witness, only know about that."

"Your secret is safe with me Claire, you know that. But it makes me wonder. Go Claire. Go; get away for a while," added Isabella.

Troy returned to the table. He announced, "Claire, Lizzie is delighted with the plan. She said to call her tonight. As luck would have it, she has off a couple a days at the end of the week. It's perfect timing."

"Thanks, Troy, that is so kind of Lizzie. I'm so glad I have caring friends like you two. Now that I have given this some thought, this is just what I needed. Thanks again guys."

"You are so welcome," chimed in Troy and Isabella.

Later that evening, Claire called Julie, a good neighbor in the building. "Hey Julie, how are you?"

"Oh, busy at work of course, but as of late not much is new. How about you, Claire?"

Claire didn't want to rehash the bizarre story. The truth of the matter was she was starting to firmly deny any of it had taken place at all. "I'm fine.

A little over worked I'd say. I planned a mini trip to Seattle and was wondering if you wouldn't mind watching over Sammy for me for a few days."

"Oh, Claire, of course not. We love Sammy. Well, Heaven is head over heels in love with Sammy. Absolutely, we would be thrilled."

Claire knew how kind Julie was and had been hoping she wasn't too busy. "Oh, thank you, Julie. Remember, anytime you need a sitter, I will take in Heaven, no problem. As a matter of fact, with your permission, I will ask Heather to walk both Heaven and Sammy next week for me." Heather, Sammy's dog walker, was a gem. Claire and Julie talked over the particulars and then said goodnight. "Thanks again Julie, I really appreciate it."

Later that same night, Claire made her plans and finished talking with Lizzie. "You are going to love coming here this week, Claire. I have off Thursday and Friday because of the school holiday. We can go to the market to enjoy some great food and we can plan to see some art galleries or maybe some museums. I am already making plans as we speak, Claire."

Claire questioned Lizzie one last time. "Are you sure you don't mind? I mean it's really short notice."

"Of course not, Claire. Now, who's going to take care of Sammy for you?"

"My friend Julie. She lives here in my building, one floor up. We have parties on the weekends sometimes and we help each other out. She loves Sammy. Best of all, she has a friend for Sammy, a mixed breed named Heaven."

"That's great, Claire. So all plans forward I say, see you Thursday morning."

"Thanks again, Lizzie, see you Thursday. Bye."

Claire tidied up the condo. The dishwasher started with the usual hesitation; the rumbling noise, which she had meant to call a repairman about. It was at the top of the list and there it would probably stay for a while. She had a list on the side of the refrigerator that seemed to grow in length faster than she could delete from it. She would definitely take care of it the minute she got back.

Chapter 2

Claire woke with a start. Her palms were sweaty, her bedclothes drenched. The dream had prevented her peaceful sleep yet again. It was only 4:45 am. This was the fourth time this week. She remembered it vividly. Walking to her destiny, she sees him. Standing a short distance away, a tall figure fully covered in a robe gestures for her to follow him. She goes with no hesitation, joyous and thankful she has found her rightful place.

From her bed, she began to look around her room. Her queen-size bed with matching bed-skirt, comforter, and pillows were shimmering in the moonlight peeking through her full-length sheer silk curtains. The antique dresser her cousin had lovingly restored stood proudly erect. Everything looked to be in its place, including her dog, Sammy, who looked up at her. "I'm fine, just had that stupid dream again, that's all, go back to sleep. Mama might as well get up."

Claire's boss, Mr. Higgins, was easygoing and let her have the rest of the week off. In addition, he said she could have off Monday and Tuesday of the following week, so she could do a couple of errands here in town once she got back. She worked at a lawyer's office as a paralegal. She worked long hours at times and was stuck in somewhat of a rut. She had been contemplating going back to school or perhaps taking the law entrance exam and pursuing law school.

Just last month she'd been forced to hire a dog sitter for Sammy, but it had worked out in the end. She had found Heather with the help of Doug, an employee at Doggie World. She'd complained she needed to get Sammy out more during the week. He told her he knew just the person to handle that problem. One week later, Claire had hired Heather on the spot, and Sammy was once again a happy dog. Heather walked Sammy every day at 1 pm and brought Sammy by to see her on Thursdays at the office. In addition, she always took Sammy to the park as much as possible, and spent the majority of every weekend with him as well.

Claire made all the necessary phone calls, and checked to make sure she didn't need an oil change yet. Now she only needed to pick up the dry cleaning, tidy up the condo, and then take Sammy over to Julie. She was positive Sammy was going to manage without her. Sammy and Claire had a close relationship, but Sammy seemed to forget about her in the presence of Heaven, go figure. That's a guy for you.

Julie ended up coming over to pick up Sammy. Sammy and Heaven played jubilantly while Julie and Claire talked. Claire gave Julie some supplies she had picked up at Doggie World along with some bones for Heaven. She gave Julie one hundred dollars and Sammy's emergency numbers, just in case. Julie reassured her all would be well and promised to call often so she could *talk* to Sammy, when suddenly, they were interrupted by the phone ringing. She picked it up on the second ring, "Hello." There was only silence on the other end. "Hello." "HELLO!" Now she could hear heavy breathing and what sounded like shoes beating the pavement.

A voice repeated, "Forgotten Caves, Forgotten Caves." More heavy breathing and what sounded like running and then only the dial tone. She hung up.

"What a jerk," she said to Julie.

"Who was it Claire?"

"I don't know who the person was. I heard heavy breathing and then he said, 'Forgotten Caves,' in a scary sort of way." *What in the world was that about?* she wondered.

"Apparently a wrong number," she said to Julie. She checked the caller ID, but all it said was "private number." Oh well, it probably was some kid. But it seemed pretty farfetched that a kid would go to the trouble to stage a stunt like that to scare her.

Claire kissed her trusty canine 49 times and left Sammy in the capable hands of Heaven. She locked up the condo and headed down to the car. Just as she was approaching the car she caught a scent of pine cones and straw. She turned around in all directions, and just as fast, the scent was gone. What the hell was that all about? Maybe she *was* too stressed out. Maybe this mini trip was exactly what she needed.

Chapter 3

She buckled herself in and concentrated on the drive. She let her worries fall away. She started to smile, emboldened by that feeling of weightlessness you experience when all is well and you're actually on vacation with nothing to worry about until your calendar tells you so smile. She listened to the oldies from the 80's and 90's. She rolled the back windows partially down and let the breeze blow through her long chestnut hair. It felt liberating. She didn't care that her hair and makeup would look worse for wear. She sang loud and swayed to the beat. She was not little by any means, standing at 5' 6" and around 135 lbs., if anyone asked, including the doctor. She carried herself well, exercised regularly, and bought local food supplies every chance she got. Good posture, good teeth, and clean underwear were important, as her aunt had instilled in her from the time she was very young.

Claire arrived at the Glad You Didn't Pass Motel a little after 8 pm. She didn't plan to meet Lizzie until

Thursday morning and thought it would be fun to stop and see her old friends, Becca and Cheryl. It was actually more of a bed and breakfast than a motel. It did have separate entrances to the outside rooms, but it had a huge main room where guests could gather and mingle, with several cozy settees and big arm chairs—all to be enjoyed beside the blazing fire in the see-through stone fireplace. The hewn oak floors had been reclaimed from an old hotel about to be demolished. It gave the room character. There were floor to ceiling wood cased windows with arched transforms on top. The chandeliers hung in various places giving off the gentle light that beckoned you to come, sit, and relax. The rich colors within added to the overall effect. This enormous room, with the oversized furniture, welcomed you.

The owners, Becca and Cheryl, were old college friends of hers, from the University of Maryland. They had always been a couple, in love since she had known them, and this motel was perfect for them. They always gave her the room with the best views of the coast, if it were at all possible.

Claire sat down in an armchair with a cherry floral pattern and picked up a gardening magazine from the end table. One article gave advice on planting Knock Out roses. Even though she didn't have a garden of her own, she loved all things related to gardening. She was so engrossed in the story, she didn't hear Cheryl approach.

"Hello Claire, Becca and I are so very glad you came to see us." They hugged and exchanged the latest news concerning their families.

"Aunt Sissy is doing fairly well—I talk to her every chance I get. My cousins are doing just great and I hope to see them both this summer," explained Claire. Cheryl told her that she and Becca were preparing to expand. They were going to open an attached restaurant with a gourmet chef no less. Claire told her that was such a bold move to make. One she was sure would eventually lead to financial security.

"We hope so, Claire. Right now it's really overwhelming. We're nervous but happy." They chatted some more and waited for Becca to join them.

Becca, the more spirited one, ran up to her from behind and hugged her. "Oh Claire, I've missed you. Cheryl and I often reminisce about all the good times we've had and discuss how we should visit each other more often. But, as you can see, our business makes us happy and sad. Business has been so hectic that sometimes we yearn to take a well-deserved vacation."

Over dinner that night, Cheryl commented on her quick decision to take a few days off. "I am truthfully a little stressed out and I needed to do this," Claire explained.

"No problem, we are delighted you are here honey, and we hope you have a wonderful time."

"Thanks Cheryl, I already am." They laughed about silly but treasured memories. For Claire, the moment felt so good, so right, she hadn't even realized she had forgotten what wonderful times they'd had together. A couple of drinks later, and a whole lot of laughter, she said goodnight.

As she walked to her room, she decided it was time to cozy up to a good book and comfy pillow. She had to brave the windy conditions, nearly losing control of her unruly dress flying about. At the doorstep, she dropped her room key and bent over to retrieve it, when the hair on the back of her neck rose. She felt—no—needed, to get in her room as fast as possible.

It was then that she heard a soft, low growling sound coming from somewhere at the edge of the woods, across from the parking lot. She shot through the door just before something slammed up against the door—hard. Her heart was in her throat, and she was too scared to look out the window. Several minutes went by. She heard nothing. It must have been something loose flying about in the wind, she told herself. But she never lied to herself, and she knew with certainty something bad had just happened.

Chapter 4

She left the next morning, having had little sleep. She thought about turning around and going home, but was too scared to, too confused. Perhaps at Lizzie's she could relax and figure things out. There had to be a reasonable explanation for everything. There just had to be.

She arrived at Lizzie's condo about two hours later. She parked on the street and gathered her coat and suitcase. She had to walk up several steps and almost dropped her purse. As she leaned over to hike her purse up higher on her shoulder, she saw Lizzie coming to the rescue.

"Hello Claire, let me help."

"Lizzie, it's so good to see you again. Thanks for taking me in, so to speak."

"Claire, we're going to have a blast."

They hugged. They walked back to the car and retrieved everything so she wouldn't have to make an additional trip. Her condo was on the 3rd floor, with sweeping views of Puget Sound.

"Oh Lizzie, your condo is exquisite. My god, it's so beautiful."

"Thanks Claire, I love it here. Come and sit down. Did you have a good trip?"

No, she thought, more like a nightmare, but all she said was, "it's great not being at work."

"I'm so excited, no one has been here to visit me since school started. I need a break from the kids, if only for a long weekend."

Claire arched her brows at the comment.

"Don't get me wrong, I love the kids and my job, but I need a small respite sometimes."

"Me too," Claire agreed.

"Do you want something to drink?"

"No thanks, but you can point me in the right direction to the bathroom."

"Sure, down the hall, first door on your right. Your room is just beyond the bathroom on the right, as well."

"Got it."

After she had set down her things she called Julie on her cell, to see if Sammy was fine. "Of course Sammy is fine; it has only been one night. He doesn't even notice you've been gone."

Claire had to laugh, "I guess Heaven has him occupied?"

"Oh yeah, they've been playing, eating, and sleeping; in that order. They only sleep after they have exhausted themselves," added Julie. "Don't worry Claire, I'll call if anything is wrong. Go, enjoy your mini vacation, all is well here." She thanked Julie and told Sammy she loved him.

Much later after having a meal fit for a queen, Claire and Lizzie decided to head over to the local café and have the best coffee Seattle had to offer. Much to her delight, the coffee hit the spot. "Mmm, this is so delicious Lizzie—nothing like a good cup of coffee."

"That's what I say too, Claire. I could never live somewhere without my coffee. I'm hooked for life."

They had fun talking with Lizzie's friends at the café. One girl, Mauri, was telling them about her recent renovation, and the efficiency of her contractors that she had found on Danny's List. Mauri said they were thorough and cleaned up every day. She showed them pictures from her phone and Claire was stunned at the before and after photos. She thought that, that was exactly what she should do to her condo. She had money saved—a substantial amount. She only splurged on Sammy, never herself.

"Hey Claire, did you hear what Mauri just said?"

"I'm sorry. No, I didn't. I was thinking that maybe I will start plans to renovate my condo when I return."

"That's a great idea Claire," said Lizzie. Then she added, "Mauri just told me she is getting married to Tom next June. Isn't that great? Tom is my second cousin no less. A wonderful man and handsome, if I say so myself."

"I say so too," added Mauri.

"I'm so happy for you, Mauri! Congratulations." Lizzie was bubbling over with enthusiasm and they happily discussed plans to be made.

After a few minutes she got up out of her chair and wandered over and sat down in the overstuffed plush wing back chair. She gazed out through the magnificent wooden bay windows near the entrance—people of all ages walking by. Going where, she pondered; so many people, seemingly in a rush. Some talking with partners, some pushing strollers, and most had a dog on a leash.

Life is ever-changing, so complicated, she thought. What was she doing? Where was she going with her life? She was sure she'd had this talk already with herself, and she knew exactly who, and what she was, and where she wanted to go. But now, she felt unsure. Like maybe she needed to reexamine herself and make a new plan forward. She vowed to do just that. Perhaps she needed to change jobs. She certainly would have more free time to visit her family and friends. Have more time for Sammy. Maybe even a relationship with that special someone. Yeah, like that was going to happen.

Oh, she dated here and there, but nothing too serious. She always lost her cool if her date would want to come up to the condo. She just couldn't move past that issue. She had no problem going to his condo, but when he asked to spend the night at hers, she broke off the relationship. She figured her time would come—maybe.

It was pleasant just looking out the window. A view of the Space Needle and the sun peeking through the clouds created a stunning view. At times like this, she felt one with the earth and sky—peaceful and calm. She would figure things out here. She decided she was very happy that she had come. This was just what the doctor ordered. She would go home soon, start making decisive choices, and move to execute her plans.

Her thoughts were interrupted with a voice from behind. "Claire honey, I'm sorry if you felt you weren't included in our discussions. Please forgive me. I just noticed you had moved off over here," exclaimed Lizzie.

"Oh, please. I am enjoying myself. I hope you are too."

"Truly you aren't mad?"

"Of course not, silly."

"Okay then, I'll just say goodbye to Mauri and we'll leave."

"Sure, take your time, I'll wait here." She turned and waved to Mauri. "I'll see you next time and good luck with your plans," she shouted.

Ten minutes later they left. Lizzie needed to stop by the dry cleaner on their way back to the condo. It was a short fifteen minute walk from the café. The walk was pleasant and cool. It cleared her mind of cobwebs and happiness stole into her soul. *I needed this,* she thought. A perfect idea—one which she intended to thank Isabella and Troy for as soon as she got home.

The next morning, as they were finishing a light breakfast, Lizzie received a phone call from her mother. Lizzie's mother said she fell down off the curb in front of the library and fractured her ankle. She insisted she was fine and that Larry, her neighbor two doors down, was taking good care of her. Lizzie, however, was still concerned. Lizzie told her mother she would be there on Sunday morning to spend the day and make sure she had everything she needed.

After she hung up, she apologized profusely to Claire, and said that she could spend the weekend in her condo anyway, taking all the time she needed and enjoying herself in the process. Claire told her she would think about it. Her mind had been made up instantly, but she didn't want to seem rude after all of Lizzie's hospitality. *We still have tomorrow to do things and I'm sure it will be fun.*

With dread and doom in the farthest part of her mind, they took off after breakfast and visited several art galleries. They stopped first at Matthews Art Gallery and thoroughly enjoyed their leisurely pace. Then, they headed over to the Alison Gallery of Art on Abrams Street. She loved looking intensely at another artists' work. She tried to imagine what the artist saw and felt as they were creating their masterpiece. She painted a little with oils, dabbled in pottery, but certainly not on the same caliber as these artists. But it gave her something. Something inside, and filled some of the emptiness she felt often, but understood—not.

They ate a late lunch, and headed back to the condo. As they sat down resting in the condo, Lizzie said, "What would you like to plan for tomorrow?"

"I'm too tired to think, my feet hurt," emphasized Claire as she rubbed her legs and feet.

"I know, I know, my feet are sore as well, Claire. I think we must have walked four hundred sixty-nine miles today. I walk a lot at school but today felt like a marathon."

"Let's just relax tonight and make our plans later," Claire said.

Lizzie curled up on the oversized couch. "Sounds good to me. Hey, why don't we just order pizza later?"

"That would be excellent."

They ended up watching a chick flick with dinner and calling it an early night.

Having made no plans, they talked over breakfast the next morning.

"I say we head over to the wharf and then have some lunch. Maybe go downtown, and do some shopping as well. What do you think, Claire?"

"That sounds fantastic," she replied. In truth, she didn't want to schedule another hectic day. She would much rather just go with whatever the moment struck. Little did she realize how fast the moment would strike.

Chapter 5

Down at the wharf, they walked around taking in the sights and sounds that are unique to Seattle— sea gulls diving around the pilings, the smell of fish in the air. The catch of the day loaded onto crates— fishermen selling their wares. It smelled like Seattle. Today, at least this morning, it wasn't even raining.

Lizzie and Claire had just arrived at the edge of the sea wall, when she heard a commotion behind her. As she turned around, she felt something strange. Like someone pushing her with their hands. It was then, that she saw a man running straight for her with savage intent in his eyes. He had his head lowered like a running back, but it was his eyes that paralyzed her. His eyes were empty and cold.

A chill coursed through her body. Before she could shake off the feeling, and react to the situation, another man ran toward her from somewhere to her left. He ran right past her, intercepted the man running straight for her, knocking him over. Both men went down in a heap. The man lying on the ground quickly shoved the stranger aside and punched him hard in the stomach. *Oomph*, the stranger grunted in pain and held his mid-section. The man with the cold eyes used that moment to his advantage; he jumped to his feet and took off running.

He disappeared around the corner. After a moment or two of stunned disbelief, she offered her hand to the stranger, and asked him if he was alright.

"Yes. Yes, I'm fine, I think. Just a little embarrassed he managed to get away."

"Get away?" she said. "I'm just glad you're not hurt." It was then that the stranger looked at Claire as if he knew her. *Why is he looking at me like that, like I'm his little sister.*

"That man looked like he was purposely going to knock you in the water, Claire," said Lizzie. She was still nervously looking in the direction the man had ran, like she was willing him not to return, to keeping running far away. She was clearly pretty shook up like Claire.

"I know, but I have never seen that man before, Lizzie. I don't understand." But, she was afraid, she was beginning to.

There were too many coincidences. How could all these situations involve her, and not be connected to her. She paid her taxes; put her trash out on time. She had her car insurance paid in full already. There were no unpaid tickets or points against her driver's license; she voted with due diligence. A good girl, really she was, she silently screamed to the heavens.

Damn. Did she have a magnet on her back? Attracting all scary people to her? They seemed to be coming out of the woodwork in droves.

"Thank you. Thank you. I can't thank you enough. Please, is there anything I can do for you? I'm sorry, what is your name sir?" asked Claire.

The stranger didn't give his name, saying he preferred not to wait for the police; apparently, he was in a rush to get to the bus stop.

She tried to thank him again, but he started backing away in haste, apologizing yet again, "for not being able to detain the aggressor."

Claire pleaded with the stranger. "Please. At least let me thank you properly. I would be happy to pay your bus fare, or buy you a cup of coffee." He politely declined but looked pleased by her insistence.

He was "quite busy," he said. "Late," he said.

Then, he too, was gone from sight.

Several passersby stopped to inquire if they were unharmed. Claire heard herself repeat several times that she was fine; that it was just an unfortunate incident. People dispersed fairly quickly, returning to their appointed slow, leisurely pace.

Lizzie insisted they call the police. Claire convinced her that perhaps they should just leave. Go have some lunch, and talk about what to make of it all. She needed to think things through.

Lizzie reluctantly agreed. They met up with Lizzie's friend, Jared, at the Sandwich Shop. They kept her talking until early afternoon.

"It was so weird, Jared. I mean that man was running straight for Claire, and he was focused only on her. I think that's why he didn't see the stranger coming up on him."

Jared said, "Why didn't you guys call the police?"

Claire jumped in. "The stranger said he didn't have time for the police, and that they couldn't do anything anyway. Lizzie wanted me to call them, but, by the time they would have arrived, everyone would have been long gone anyway."

"You still should have called the police, what if this psychopath followed you?" added Jared as he slowly looked around at the patrons. At this, Claire and Lizzie slowly looked around the room too. People of all ages, races, and cultures were here—a melting pot, representing the diversity that unified them all.

"I think he was probably just high on drugs or something, Jared." That earned a frown on both of their faces. *I'm getting seriously scared. What if someone gets hurt because some crazy guy is after me?*

Things were escalating at an alarming rate. What was she going to do? Who was she going to turn to for help? With thoughts and questions racing through her head, she didn't hear Jared.

He said rather loudly, "Hello, Claire, where are you?"

"What, I'm sorry. I seem to be lost in thought lately. What did you say?"

"I said a friend of mine is a detective on the police force. I could call him right now. Invite him to meet us over at the café, if you would like."

"I mean, I would love to meet your friend, but I don't see the need really."

"Let's head over to the café, I'll call and see if he's available." They found parking a short distance from the café, right before it started to drizzle.

By the time they had settled into their seats, it had genuinely started to rain. About ten minutes later, Jared introduced his friend, Mike, as he came over to their table.

"Claire, this is my good friend, Detective Mike Jordan."

"Hello, thanks so much for coming. I told Jared and Lizzie not to bother you."

"Are you kidding? Jared is paying tonight, so I'm all ears." That comment sent Jared and Lizzie into laughing mode. Claire didn't understand why they were laughing until she glanced at his ears. They were much larger than the average sized ears. They were humungous and they stuck out at a funny angle. She immediately felt trite when she realized he was aware she was staring.

"It's alright, Claire, I love my large ears. And all my lady friends love them too!"

"Sure. You wish, Mike," said Jared. "Whenever we go out together, no one notices you with me to look at."

That sort-of broke the ice. Claire felt much more at ease for the moment. That is until Mike appeared ready to listen to her story, as crazy as it was.

After ordering a double latte and a huge slice of carrot cake, Mike was ready to listen.

"So tell me from the beginning, Claire."

She was hesitant to tell everyone at the table the whole story. She weighed her options. They were all looking at her and she got the distinct impression they knew she was debating how much to reveal.

Mike spoke up. "Claire, perhaps we should go somewhere more private."

"No, Mike. I'm just unsure what to say, it all seems so ridiculous. You're going to think I'm a nut case."

"No, I won't. Just start at the beginning, Claire," reiterated Mike.

Mike took out a small notebook and began writing.

"Well, after leaving work early last week, I decided to stop by the park. I stayed too late, and finally noticed everyone was gone. I became scared all of a sudden, like someone was watching me. I felt someone watching me, so I ran to my car. I didn't ever actually see anyone, but I knew somehow, someone was there, and focused on me. See, even to me it sounds nutty." She looked around the table at her friends. She saw questioning looks on their faces.

Mike spoke, "You said you *felt* someone following you?"

"I didn't mean it literally, just that I got goose bumps on my arms." She quickly decided to be more careful in her responses.

"Go on Claire," prodded Mike.

"So to continue, I went to the café in town and told Troy and Isabella about my experiences. They both thought a little time off would be just what the doctor ordered. Troy called Lizzie so I could get a little R&R here. Troy is Lizzie's brother. On the way here, I stopped at my friend's motel to spend the night. I wanted it to be a relaxing, non-rushed trip. I spent a wonderful evening with my friends." Claire took a few sips of her delicious raspberry-lemonade drink.

"As I was approaching my room after dinner, I heard this low growling sound coming from across the street. I barely had time to close the door before something big and hard slammed up against the door. I was too scared to look out the window, but now I wish I had. Then today, down at the wharf, a man started running straight toward me. His eyes were locked onto me. I was so stunned by the look of malice in his eyes; I didn't have time to react. But a stranger intercepted him and they both landed hard on the ground. The man punched the stranger that helped me, and disappeared around the corner." Claire looked at her friends to gauge their reaction thus far. The story was so implausible that she had to remind herself it really happened.

"Soon after the scuffle, I helped the stranger up and asked if he was okay. He said something I didn't expect. He said he was sorry that the man got away. I was just so relieved he wasn't hurt, but he seemed more concerned with me. When Lizzie wanted to call the police he started backing away, said he was in a hurry. That's pretty much it."

"Okay, do you have a description of the two men, Claire?" asked Detective Jordan.

"Hmm. Let's see, the man running toward me was perhaps 5'10", approximately 160-170 lbs., with dark brown hair and cold black eyes. I remember the eyes well. Other than that, I'm really not sure how else to describe him. He looked trim and fit, but I was in a bit of a shock to remember much else. It all happened so fast. It seemed surreal to me."

"Alright, that's good Claire. Let me know if you remember anything else," said Detective Jordan.

"Okay. Lizzie, your turn," said Detective Jordan. "Start with the stranger."

Lizzie looked like she was concentrating as she said; "the stranger was about 5'10" - 5'11", about 150 lbs., with green eyes I think."

"That's great Lizzie; now tell me about the man running toward Claire," said Detective Jordan.

Lizzie squinted as she said, "He was around 5'10", approximately 160 to 180 lbs., and he had dark hair and dark eyes."

Detective Jordan looked somewhat puzzled. "Are you sure he was running straight for Claire?

Perhaps he was running away from something or someone."

"It was bizarre Mike; I believe he had every intention of harming Claire. He never even glanced my way, and I was standing right beside her."

Mike closed his notebook. "I'm not sure what I can do, but I will go down to the wharf and look around, ask a few questions. See what I can dig up. Leave me your contact information, Claire. I will get in touch with you as soon as I know something."

He saw the far away, forlorn look she had. He tried to reassure her. "If there's anything more to this incident, I promise you, I will give it my full attention."

"Thank you so very much, Mike. I don't know how to thank you." She felt relieved that Detective Jordan would be helping her. She was feeling somewhat helpless. She needed to understand what, exactly, was going on.

"Listen, you can buy me dinner sometime. I'm partial to lobster." They all laughed.

"It's a deal. Thanks again, I know you're busy."

Shortly thereafter, Mike left and they walked over to the car. Jared had to go in a different direction but offered to drop them off at the condo. Lizzie and Claire firmly declined. They actually *wanted* to walk all the way to their door. Somehow, they felt the *need* to return to a normal routine. It was important not to be afraid. There were plenty of people on the streets at this hour, and plenty of dogs as well. Dogs liked Claire. She considered herself a dog person. You know, the type of person dogs felt comfortable around. No quick movements. No petting unless she had introduced herself first, and had silently asked for permission to love on him or her. Claire was sure that the dogs would rally around her should she cry for help. But all seemed quiet and tranquil, at least for now.

"Lizzie, Claire, I think it would be best if I dropped you guys off. I would be worried sick if you both walked home from here."

Claire spoke first. "Jared, clearly you are a wonderful, thoughtful, friend. The events today have gravely affected both of us but I believe I speak for both of us when I say we need to feel safe again. Safe to walk down the street and go about our business, like we would normally every day. I don't know how to put into words what I know I need, but the best way I can describe it, is to say that, if we can no longer walk down the street, then whoever did this wins."

"I couldn't have said it better myself," added Lizzie.

He shook his head in acknowledgment. He hugged them and insisted Lizzie must call him after they arrived back at her house.

They had an uneventful walk back and Lizzie called the minute they got in, as promised. Thankful, they took a rest for an hour, ate a light dinner, and discussed their plans.

She knew it was time to leave. She didn't want Lizzie in any danger because of her, or anyone else for that matter. She told Lizzie of her decision to leave in the morning the same time Lizzie was to leave to go take care of her mother.

"Oh Claire, I feel awful. Please feel free to stay and rest, leave anytime you want to."

"Thanks, Lizzie, and I really mean it. I have had a wonderful time. Truly, I have. I just think I'll go home and start planning my renovations. I need to focus on something else. I have a few errands to take care of, and I need to do some making up to Sammy as well. Work is probably piling up, and I might as well go back to work early. I don't know, I'll just see how it goes."

Later that night, she went over everything that had happened. She needed to talk to her family. Her family consisted of two cousins and an aunt. A little dysfunctional, but they were all she had, and she adored them. She would wait until she got back home and settled in before she placed the call. She would sugar coat the scary parts, and ask for advice. They stayed in touch and held each other up, so to speak.

Her cousin, Jacqueline, had stayed with Claire when she first moved in. For three weeks, she had helped her with the unpacking and decorating. Jacqueline, an interior designer, had designed a beautiful bedroom for Claire on the cheap.

Another cousin, Brooke, who owned her own antique store, had sent many special pieces for Jacqueline to incorporate in her design. The end result had been spectacular.

Aunt Sissy, who Claire loved with all her heart, was sadly a little fragile these days. She decided that she should probably only discuss this problem with her cousins. It might upset Aunt Sissy too much.

Chapter 6

The next morning they hugged, promised to stay in touch, and then parted ways. Lizzie waited until Claire drove off to get in her car and leave. The drive home was exhausting. She was nervous and kept checking her rear view mirror to see if she was being followed. She stopped once to eat at a little Mom and Pop diner right off the interstate. It was called Sal's Home of the Footlong.

She parked and quickly made her way inside, fearful for the first time of the walk from her car to the restaurant. She ordered a chili dog with cheese fries. Enjoying a few minutes of peace, she ate her food in sweet silence, feeling full and content until she exited the door, that is.

Beyond was a vast expanse of wasteland between her and the car. Her view seemed skewed. The car seemed to take on a life of its own just daring her to step off the curb and follow. Virtually anyone could be hiding between the parked cars, or just behind the corner of the building. Perhaps the man sitting on his Harley casually talking on his cell phone was a lookout. Instantly her feelings of normalcy were replaced with apprehension.

The once beautiful everyday scenery that she loved no matter if it were trees or desert, water or land, now was replaced with shadows of doom, waiting abductors, creepy crawly things that go boo in the dark. Feeling the world closing in on her, her world was like a tunnel from the door to the car. That was her mission; get to the car, with terror waiting to overtake her should she falter. She forced herself to walk all those heavy laden foot falls that seemed to take forever. Each step brought her closer, yet with each step it seemed harder to take another until she finally arrived at the car door. She jumped back quite suddenly, nearly falling over after remembering previous news reports a few years back. Around Christmas time, some people would lie under cars and prey on unsuspecting victims, grabbing their ankles as they would unlock their car door, quickly overtaking them as they tried to get up. Claire peered cautiously under the car and saw no one, so she climbed in and drove straight home with no incidents.

Sammy was overjoyed to see her. He was jumping up and down, trying to get into her arms, so she crouched down and let him have his fill. Meanwhile,

Julie told her all about their adventures and how cute Sammy and Heaven were together. Julie exclaimed she would happily watch Sammy anytime. Julie fished out the money and house key from her purse.

Claire demanded she keep both. "I appreciate you watching Sammy and I would prefer you keep the key and the money in case of an emergency."

They lightly argued. Julie finally gave up and said she would keep the money. She would store it with the key for some unforeseen emergency. Julie said she had already taken the dogs to the park for over an hour and Sammy was good and tired. So, Claire and Sammy went home and rested for the rest of the evening.

Surrounded by her things, the things that were familiar and comforting, gave her a false sense of security she was totally willing to accept. Sammy would warn her of any would-be intruders. No one could bother her here.

Lizzie called on Monday. "I have some bad news," she said softly.

Claire was immediately alarmed. "What is it? Is your mother alright?"

"Yes, she's fine. It's Detective Jordan, Claire. I don't know all the details, but his house was burned down, and Mike was not able to escape in time."

"Oh my god. Oh, my, god." She couldn't think of anything else to say. Her mind was racing with the possible implications. "I'll drive back tomorrow morning, Lizzie."

"No, I know you have to go back to work. I'm okay, really. Jared is distraught by the circumstances, though. All of his close friends will make sure he has the support he needs. Detective Jordan's family will be arriving in town tomorrow and the funeral will be later in the week."

"I'm so very sorry, Lizzie. I don't know what to say. It's such a tragic loss. I had only just met him but I immediately liked him. He was funny and sweet." There was a swift intake of breath on the other end. Lizzie was struggling to contain herself. "When you get more details please let me know. And, please tell me the address of the funeral home as soon as you know it, so I can send flowers."

"Sure, Claire, I knew you would want to know." They talked for a few more minutes and then said their goodbyes.

She walked over to retrieve her phone. She played back the message from Detective Jordan. Somehow she had missed the call, and only thought about checking her messages after she had arrived home.

"Claire, this is Detective Jordan. I just wanted to briefly let you know I have made some progress in the case. I need to talk with you as soon as possible. I no longer believe this was a random attack. Please call me on my cell phone as soon as possible."

She called him numerous times and left several messages with no response. Now she knew why. Was this an accident pure and simple, or was it somehow connected to her? She didn't want to believe it could be connected to the incident down at the wharf, but she was afraid she wouldn't like the answer.

She decided that she would ask Julie to watch Sammy and the condo again, just for a week or so. She arranged the pet sitter for both Heaven and Sammy, and paid a month in advance. She needed to go back to Seattle and end this somehow. It felt right. It took her a few days to make all the arrangements. Her boss was confused by her explanation to take a leave of absence, but approved it anyway, because he said he didn't want to lose her.

The drive to Seattle was thankfully uneventful. She gassed up and made sure her windshield washer fluid was full before she left, so she wouldn't have to stop in route. Not being able to help herself, she constantly checked her surroundings. Taking note of the type and color of the cars around her, she tried to remember each one to see if the cars would still be behind her miles down the road. It was mentally exhausting. She checked in at a hotel downtown, and then called Lizzie. "Hello Lizzie, it's Claire."

"Hello, how are you doing, Claire? I'll be going to the funeral later today." She sounded how Claire felt, so sad, so lost for words.

"Actually, Lizzie, I'm not at home. I drove up today because I would like to attend Detective Jordan's funeral, if possible."

"Of course, it's at Damien's Funeral Home on Second Street. The service is at two o'clock. Come on over, I hope you brought an overnight bag so you can spend the night. You can have the guest bedroom, no problem."

"No thanks, Lizzie. I already checked in at the Wyatt."

"Why didn't you call me? You know I have plenty of room at my place."

"I didn't want to invite myself. Anyway, I'm comfortable here at the hotel and you are back to work now. I'm sure you're busy. Really Lizzie, I'm fine here. We'll get together."

"Okay, if you're really sure," said Lizzie.

"I'm sure," replied Claire.

Chapter 7

Claire knew someone would be there, watching, waiting.

She gave her condolences to his mother and father. They seemed inconsolable, so lost. His parents were flanked on both sides by his siblings. His sister was crying uncontrollably, while her husband whispered comforting words into her ear. She was a boiling cauldron of anger. She was so angry that someone had killed him.

Claire knew that it was not an accident as the pastor so eloquently put it. "A tragedy," he said. "God must have needed him," he said.

She was full of rage. She wanted to storm to the podium and tell the gathered mourners that someone or something had murdered Detective Jordan. She wanted to assure them she would avenge his murder. That she would mete out a small measure of justice. But she knew she had little chance of that. She knew she was probably not going to live long herself. She had no idea what this person or persons wanted from her. What would be demanded of her if she survived the week?

The cars wound their way through the cemetery until they came to an area that had been prepared. There were three rows of seats for the family members. She stood off to the side as words were said, and flowers were laid across the casket. Lizzie and Jared came over to stand beside her. They stood in silence for a few minutes. She felt the guilt swamping all her senses, like a fog that was engulfing her. It was irrational. But it was a ball and chain pulling her down. She wanted, no needed, to kill the bastard. She reflected on the fact that life was not fair and far too short.

Jared spoke first. "Lizzie, I miss him. He was a good friend."

Claire added, "I would give anything to buy him that lobster dinner I owed him."

"I didn't want to tell you guys before the funeral, but I just found out some disturbing news," said Jared. "Jim Eanes, he's on the police force and was good friends with Mike, bumped into me at the coffee shop this morning. He told me that the autopsy report indicated that Mike's windpipe was crushed. He died before the fire took place. The fire was just to cover up the murder."

It was murder then, just as Claire had suspected. Someone had killed him and then had tried to cover it up. Now she knew she was in real trouble here. Feeling bold and angered earlier, she felt scared now. She might very well end up the same, and soon. She needed help; she was way in over her head. If they killed Detective Jordan, what would they do to her?

Detective Jordan had deserved so much better. Not knowing how long he knew—that moment in time when you just know. You know all options are over, there is no preventing it, it will happen. How long did he have to think about all the things worth thinking about at a time like that? Did he think about his loving parents and siblings, or did he think about things left undone that he wanted to finish before he left? Perhaps, he had used his last moments on this land, forgiving of those who held ill will toward him. Maybe he had done none of those things. Maybe he had used his last moments to calmly accept what he could not change, with only a silent goodbye.

"It's not public knowledge, he told me in confidence. I didn't want his parents to find out about it today. They have enough sadness today. The news will be heart wrenching for them."

"Who would do such a thing? He was so nice," said Lizzie.

"Someone who didn't really know Mike Jordan, the man," replied Jared. "He was my best friend." Jared couldn't hold back the slight hitch in his tone as he became overwrought with grief. "He planned to buy a Mustang this year. He'd always wanted one; saved up almost nine thousand dollars. We were planning to take a trip out east next summer in his new car. Now we'll never take that trip together."

Lizzie hugged Jared for support. "He will stay in my heart and I will not forget him. Late at night, when I am content with my wandering thoughts, I will remember, and I will smile," said Lizzie.

Jared had to let her go—turning around to be alone, lost in his own thoughts for a moment, gathering his strength so he wouldn't break down.

Claire hugged Lizzie as she cried softly on her shoulder. Claire and Jared exchanged looks of sorrow; they were all choked up and couldn't talk for a few minutes.

They left shortly thereafter. Everyone was quietly dispersing. A waiting limo whisked the family members away. With their backs to the freshly dug grave, Claire watched as the departing mourners held onto their jackets and hats. A brisk breeze was blowing and the cloud cover left a shadow cast over the site that seemed all the more dreary and mournful.

Lizzie wanted her to come over with Jared to her house, but she firmly declined. She pleaded a headache and a need to rest. Lizzie said nothing, because they all understood it was a lie.

She could not expose Lizzie to any more danger. She already had Detective Jordan on her conscience. After taking her leave, she drove two blocks over then doubled back and drove close to his gravesite. Pulling over, she sat there in the car for twenty minutes. Then a somewhat now familiar push prompted her to prepare to leave. Someone had arrived.

As she pulled away from the curb she spotted someone walking toward the car in her rear-view mirror. The person was wearing a hoodie so she couldn't ascertain if it was a male or female. She slowed to a stop and leaned out the window to get a better look at the person walking steadily toward her car until she saw what was under the hoodie. It was then she pushed down on the accelerator as far as it would go. Sheer terror propelled her, for under the hoodie, she saw total blackness. No discernible face was there. As she spun out, she glanced in the rear view mirror. The form, for she couldn't call it anything else, was still moving casually in the direction of the car.

She didn't know what to do, where to go, how far to run. She drove in a general direction away from the form, and that was her only goal for the moment. As she pulled off the interstate and slowed down, eventually coming to a halt at the stoplight, she knew she needed to have a more concrete plan if she were to have any hope of surviving. She nervously looked around at the occupants in the surrounding cars. They seemed normal to her, but what did she know? Any of these people could be following her, waiting for the right moment to attack, or worse. She needed help as soon as possible.

The once beautiful surroundings had become ominous and scary. She couldn't see the green trees or the wild flowers still in bloom. The hanging baskets alongside the lampposts hung in their glory unseen. Two squirrels having a squabble nearly got run over as they attempted to cross the street.

A motorist broke her spell when she blasted her horn. Claire had absentmindedly drifted over into the next lane. She quickly corrected her error then waved her hand apologetically. *Focus Claire, focus.*

Looking down at her dashboard, she realized

she was riding on E. She saw a gas station up ahead on the left and decided to fill up. As she was about to make the left hand turn, she noticed a gas station further up on the right that offered regular gasoline for five cents cheaper. She quickly pulled out of the median, and made a sharp turn to the right. As she did so, a black sedan two cars back did the same, and she promptly took note of it. She decided to make a U-turn at the next light, and go to the original gas station she had picked out, because it was well lit and full of people, fitted with a mini ice cream shop within the Gas and Go. The black sedan did the same maneuver. She was being pursued by the occupants in the black sedan. She pulled in next to the pump, grabbed her purse, and ran into the shop.

"Yes ma'am, can I help you?" asked the cashier.

"Fifty on pump six please."

After paying in cash, Claire saw that no one got out of the sedan. It had parked in a space nearest to the pumps, but had backed into the space. Claire could only see three hooded heads in the car. That was proof enough for Claire. She thought about knocking on the door of the sedan as she headed out the door, but when she got closer to the sedan, she lost her nerve and quickly made her way over to her own car. She felt the persons in the black sedan following her back to the car. It made her shiver, but she refused to run. Back out on the road, Claire aimlessly drove around town, with the black sedan never far behind.

Chapter 8

Claire was running out of ideas when she spotted an antique mall show. It was the perfect solution. She would get lost in the crowd, and then make her way back to the car, or perhaps catch a taxi to the police station. Perhaps she could simply talk to the people, men, forms, whatever they were, and ask them to leave her alone. Tell them that she should not be involved in any of this, that they must have the wrong girl because she led a sane, slow, boring life. Surely they would be reasonable. Yes, she was good at making people see the reasonable side of things. They would apologize and let her be. Yeah and maybe pigs would fly.

She parked in the garage and proceeded to race across the street. She ran into the plaza that housed a multitude of shops and tried to blend into the crowd flowing amongst the antique market vendors that had taken over every available empty space. Holding a 1950's comic book in front of her face, she immediately spotted two individuals coming into the plaza that looked out of place. Rather than jeans and casual dress, they stood out from the crowd. They wore identical khaki pants and polo shirts. But that by itself was not what caught her attention. It was the fact that they had identical eyes. Slightly larger eyes than she had ever seen, with gray, aquamarine irises. They scanned the crowd, not paying any attention to the goods on the display tables.

Safety in numbers she thought. She had but a few brief minutes of ease, before she realized she had not thought this out thoroughly. There were no additional exits except for the doors she had walked through and the men took note of it. She knew the moment they had determined that and were silently communicating with each other to take up positions around the entrance.

All they needed to do now was patiently wait. Claire leaned over the table and asked the gentleman what time was closing. He politely said, "six o'clock tonight, ma'am."

"Thank you," she replied and moved on, not wanting to stand in one place for too long.

As she walked down the row of tables, she noticed a vendor up ahead that had a cane behind his chair. The vendor seemed very pleased to sell her his cane. She bought it for one hundred fifty dollars cash and quickly moved on. She spotted a vendor that had coats, hats, and various other items for sale. Fifteen minutes later, she had assembled a haphazard disguise. It was the best she could do under the circumstances, she told herself. She found a water fountain and wiped off all her makeup and took off her earrings. She found a stray rubber band on a nearby table and used it to tie her hair back, stuffing it in the hat. She didn't have a mirror to check herself, but she knew time was running out.

She had to try to leave now. She shifted to her left at the same time a man was turning, and they collided into each other.

He apologized. "Did I hurt you?"

"No, no harm done."

"Are you certain?" asked the gentleman.

"Yes, I'm terribly sorry. It was totally my fault. I wasn't paying attention. I'm distracted, trying to contemplate my predicament." She started to walk on toward the next table of wares.

"Oh really, well, is there anything I could help you with, pretty lady?"

She stopped. "I do find myself in need of a favor."

"Why anything, sugar," he answered with wandering eyes.

"I need someone to walk me to my car you see."

"Why, it would be my pleasure."

As they walked somewhat awkwardly toward the door, she spotted one of the men. She placed her hand on the arm of the man walking next to her. He took the cue, and placed her arm around his, holding tightly. He smiled down at her. She gave him her most alluring smile, and looked at him as they passed through the entrance. She waited until they were headed toward the garage, before she dared to glance around. Her pursuers were nowhere in sight. Thankful she had bumped into this man, she tried to think of a graceful way to say goodbye.

As they entered the garage the man said, "What level honey?"

"Level two. My car is just up ahead," she gestured in the general direction, when she spotted a man standing around her car looking in the window. "Oh my, I forgot, this isn't the right level."

"Huh," the man said.

He appeared to be thinking things through. He halted walking and looked at Claire. "Honey what's going on here; do you even have a car in this garage? Is this some kind of setup or something?"

Anxiously walking away, and trying to pull the man with her, Claire said, "Please. Please I'll explain later, please, let's just walk down a level. I think my car is there." Panic was setting in. The man near her car was bound to hear the commotion.

"Look, tell me what is going on here, or I will walk away right now. Hell, I don't even know your name. My name is Alan by the way."

Talking softly and still pulling him along she replied, "Nice to meet you, Alan, my name is Claire. There is a man near my car I'd rather not meet tonight, so please, just come with me. I'll call for a taxi or something."

Suddenly, with a loud thud, Alan was struck from behind. He crumpled to the floor. The man standing behind him looked big and mean.

Looking to her left, Claire saw the fire alarm. She yanked on the fire alarm and starting running. Heart pounding, she dared not look back. She could hear the man following, and he was closing in. Scared to get trapped in the elevator, she elected to take the stairs instead. As luck would have it, a couple was just entering the stairwell. Claire screamed, "rape" as loud as she could. She looked pleadingly at the couple. The man pushed his companion behind him, and sucker punched the pursuing man in the face as he bounded down the stairs. Claire kept running down the flight of stairs, and practically flew out of the door.

She didn't look back until she had passed several blocks. She sat down on the bench at the bus stop, heaving from the unfamiliar exertion. She tried to slow down her breathing while she looked around. She didn't have her car, but somehow she had managed to keep her purse. She pulled out her cell phone and called a local taxicab company to pick her up.

She stopped to buy a few necessities, then returned to her hotel and took a shower. She really hoped, no, prayed, that Alan was okay, along with the nice couple from the stairwell. She couldn't have another man's demise imprinted on her conscience.

She tried to formulate a plan. She just didn't know where to start and whom she could trust. On top of that, she would be risking the life of anyone she called. Hell, none of this made sense. For over twenty years she'd had a normal life. If there ever was such a thing, she knew she'd had it—school, college, full-time employment, a condo, a dog, etc., etc., etc. Normal, right? She was pretty sure. She was exhausted, and her head hurt from thinking too much. Finally, after thinking for way too long, but not long enough to unravel the mystery that was now her reality, she fell asleep on the arm of the chair.

The next morning she woke up at 5 o'clock. She quickly showered, dressed, packed, and headed downstairs. As she was exiting the stairwell she saw a police officer at the counter. She quickly averted her face and looked in the other direction. As she neared, she heard the desk clerk say, "Ms. Claire Richards is registered to Room 205, officer. Our records indicate she is due to check out this morning.

She slipped inside the Ladies Room, waited five or six minutes and then gingerly opened the door. The hotel clerk was busy helping another customer. It was a woman with a crying baby in her arms. She didn't see the police officer anywhere in her line of vision, so she opened the door, and continued on through the lobby doors. Striding as casually as possible, she saw the patrol car parked out front as she walked by. Thankfully, no one was inside. She walked as fast as she dared around the side of the building.

She would be too conspicuous carrying a small overnight bag down the street at 6:30 in the morning, so she moved to a stand of trees across the street. Soon, she saw the police car pull out, and move slowly down the block. She waited until after dawn, until traffic started to flow at a steady pace, and then walked down the road and three blocks over. She called for a taxicab. She headed directly to a branch bank, and withdrew eight thousand dollars in cash. Then she headed over to a used car dealership and purchased a used car from Mo Mar, a used car salesman, who promised you would get, "Mo Car For Your Money."

Chapter 9

She drove near the antique mall show just to see if anything was happening. The scene looked like the everyday normal routine taking place with people walking in and out of the antique mall show; even the garage had returned to normalcy. She wanted to retrieve her car and ditch the ratty car she had purchased but was afraid to enter the garage to see if it was still there. Instead, she decided to get something to eat and make some phone calls.

At the very next light she had a bad feeling she was being watched. After going around basically the same blocks for twenty minutes, it was apparent she was being followed. *How stupid, you just had to go back to the antique mall show.* No time to wallow in self-pity now; it was time to go.

Racing to get somewhere safe from whoever was pursuing her, she had this notion to stop the car, walk to the lot across the street, and hide behind the dumpster. Now she thought—right now. She quickly parked, grabbed her purse, and took off running behind the dumpster. *Behind the dumpster—hurry*. She did as her conscience directed, not really understanding at all, and wondering if she would be put in a home for disabled minds because of her antics.

As she hid, she slowly and carefully looked from behind the dumpster, only to see two people looking her car over. One man opened the car door and examined the interior, while the other man walked around the car and then started scanning the surroundings in all directions. She pulled her head back and quietly remained there for several minutes until her nerves made her peek again.

Nothing. The men were gone. But where were they? Oh, why did she get so scared? All the movies she had ever seen never portrayed the girl who got away as a scaredy-cat. Only the brave ones got away. This was different. She wasn't in a movie, and she couldn't turn the channel. She needed to know where they went. What if they were hiding just like she was, and were patiently waiting for her to return?

She didn't even get a good look at them. She wouldn't be able to give a decent description to the police, *if,* she went to the police. What would she say? "Some ruffians were looking at my car, officer." Okay, that would go over well. She would be on record as loony.

She looked down at her hands. They were shaking slightly. She wasn't cut out for this stuff. She wanted it all to go away. She didn't understand what was happening to her. *This is insane. I want to wake up from my nightmare.*

Looking carefully around, she tried to move her feet, but they refused to move. She was too terrified to move. She knew there was a lot of open ground back to her car. A couple of empty looking warehouses were on each side of the dumpster. At least she could see a UPS center down the street, on the corner. It seemed busy. If the men were still around, she could make tracks for the UPS center, screaming all the way. Decision made, she slowly walked around from behind the dumpster, and started toward her car.

All of a sudden, something jumped in front of her.

"Ahhhh," she yelped. She jumped so high she thought she must have hurt something. Looking down, she saw the cutest kitty cat ever.

"Hey buddy, you shouldn't do that," Claire said nervously as she darted in all directions.

"Meow," is only the response she got.

"Well, I can't leave you here; you look hungry and alone."

"Meow."

"Ok, your name is Sunny, because you are helping me forget my current life threatening situation." She scooped the cat up and walked nervously toward her car.

"Meow."

The car seemed to be at least five football fields away. By the time she got back to the car, she had broken out in a fine sweat.

Sunny sat quietly while Claire tried to decide where to go. Somehow, she knew to go to the warehouse down and around the corner; the one with the huge wooden doors. She knew this, but how did she know it? She had never, ever, visited this part of town.

She drove down the street to the location of the empty looking warehouse. There were big empty barrels in front. They were metal with a heavy rust coating on the majority of the outside. She focused on the barrels for some reason. They looked empty, but one of them she couldn't quite see in from the car. She pulled forward a little, inch by inch, trying to see into the last barrel. Something wasn't right about the last barrel.

Sunny started to hiss. She put the car in reverse and started to back up. It was then that she felt the windshield buckling and moving inward. Sunny hissed and raised her back. She accelerated as fast as she could, but a ringing in her ears was getting unbearable. When she reached the crossroad she gunned her car forward, got to the next intersection, and hung left toward the busy part of town. The windshield was restored to its normal shape, and the ringing in her ears had ceased.

Sunny settled down and she was left to wonder if it had even taken place. No one looked at her weird at the stop light. She continued on until she pulled into a fast food drive-thru. She ordered 3 chicken sandwiches, grilled, and some fries. "One milk, and one coke to go please," she added. She and Sunny sat in the parking lot munching down their food, when her cell phone rang. It was another private number calling. She thought twice about answering, but her curiosity got the better of her.

"Hello, who is this?!!!" she demanded.

"Come back to the warehouse, Claire, I will be waiting." Then the caller hung up. The voice had been that of a male. He had spoken with a very calm and passive voice. One which was neither scary nor aggressive, but by the very nature of the events thus far, she was terrified beyond imagining. How did this man know her?

This was too much—too much. Normal people like her didn't have things like this happen to them. She wanted to scream. She wanted to shout. But mostly she wanted to cry, and curl up in a ball.

Who to call? She could call her Aunt Sissy. She lived in Newark. She had helped raise her after her mother had passed away, when she was only five years old. But Aunt Sissy had early stages of dementia and she had a caregiver that lived with her.

She called Aunt Sissy. She picked up on the first ring. "Claire, honey, go to the warehouse. You need help with this, and you need it now."

"OMG, what in the world, you know? You know? What the hell is going on here, tell me," she shouted. "I have a right to know."

"Claire, I can't. Go now, and it will become clear, honey. I'm so sorry. I'm so sorry. I love you, Claire. Forever and always honey." She hung up and left Claire with her mouth hanging wide open.

She was stunned by the revelation that somehow her whole life as she had known it up to this point was looking more and more like it had been all one big sham. In that moment she felt so betrayed by the aunt she had always loved. She felt awful having yelled at her Aunt. She had never done so. She owed Aunt Sissy her life, and she had yelled at her sick

Aunt, who was maybe not so sick after all. But she had known, dammit, and she had kept it from her—whatever *it* was.

She left Sunny alone for a few minutes and ran inside to go to the restroom. She came back quickly and took Sunny over to a secluded area, with a patch of grass and trees. After a few minutes, Sunny caught on, and knew what to do. "Good girl, Sunny," although she wasn't aware if Sunny was actually a girl.

They drove back in the direction of the warehouse. She didn't turn right on Howard Avenue, but turned on Hazel Street instead. It ran parallel to the street with the warehouse Aunt Sissy told her to return to.

She was stalling. "Just go there and find out Claire," she whispered to herself. "Everything will make sense, and then my nice, normal life will be restored," she assured herself. If her nice, normal life was restored, never again would she complain.

She would have Sunny and Sammy, all her friends, and of course her job. She needed to get back to work. Next time she arrived at work she wouldn't participate in the usual banter in the mornings. Her and her co-workers liked to have a short pity party; complaining about management, pay, vacation, the price of coffee and gas, and so on. She had bills to pay and a renovation she needed to get started. She didn't have time for wild goose chases that could get her hurt, or worse.

What was she doing? She looked upward, toward the sky, but no heart stopping inspiration hit her. She had to know what was going on, and the only way she knew to find out, was to go to this seemingly empty warehouse. Maybe she should go buy a gun first or something—anything. And maybe, she would meet up with those men again. And maybe, this time they would kill her with her own gun. They did want to kill her.

Driving slowly toward the same entrance she had been to earlier, she saw no one and Sunny was quiet now. Pulling forward, she nervously looked around. The barrels were nowhere in sight. She parked. Finally, she got out of the car and carried Sunny in her arms across the small parking lot to the door. It was slightly ajar so she pushed it forward. It was a heavy, older, wooden door. The kind that squeaked loudly as it moved inward.

"Hello Claire."

A man in his late 40s or early 50s, with average height and blonde hair, motioned for her to follow him toward the back of the warehouse. He was wearing jeans and a polo shirt.

She didn't follow him. He stopped walking and turned to her.

"We don't have much time, and you need to be brought up to speed—unless you *want* the Ones to actually get their hands on you."

"I don't know any Ones, and I don't know you," she replied.

"Yes, you do. You just don't remember."

"Well then, Mr. I Know You But Just Don't Remember, I'm not going anywhere with you. You have five minutes to explain, or I am leaving."

He said nothing, just stared at her. Her heart was thudding so loud she was sure he could hear it, because he sort of cocked his head to the side. She could tell he had made a decision of some sort. Two women came from somewhere to her left, and appeared with two chairs. They were wearing identical clothing. They looked like joggers in their spandex pants and running shoes. But she noticed they had something in one ear each and she didn't think they were hearing aids. They were more like blue tooth devices, yet somewhat different. She had never seen anything like it. As she thought on this, one woman offered her a chair, while the other offered it to the man.

"Can I get you something to drink, Claire," the woman asked.

"No thank you, I won't be staying long."

Chapter 10

A chosen one—it was all designed long ago. Humans waiting until it was time—hiding her really. She was not a savior. She was not anybody's hero. She was an average, plain Jane—meandering through life with her narrow-minded goals, dammit. She didn't want any of this. She wanted her life back. She wallowed in self-pity. She embraced it even, but reality wouldn't go away. She cried for the parents she never really knew; all her family taken from her. She cried for the injustice of it all. The tears fell silently. She let them flow; maybe they would wash away the pain. The pain was so deep, so severe, she wasn't sure she would ever be the same.

They wanted her to be someone else, someone she didn't know. All things known to be truths were now questioned, all facts just theories. Who could she really trust? Crying would not change what was, but the human side of her didn't care. Her life up until the Ones came along had mattered, and she cried for the insanity of it all. Who was she? Where did she belong? They were asking things of her she didn't know if she was strong enough to give. She didn't really know if she even wanted to give to these people. They were demanding her very soul.

Chapter 11

Looking out the window of her room, she saw men and women who were training outside far below. She now lived in a safe house. Not a house, really more like a sprawling estate. It had over five hundred acres and multiple large houses along with a few warehouses that were fully operational with the most high-tech gadgets she had ever seen. Then there were garages that looked more like baseball fields and the huge forty-seven room *house* she was currently living in. Her life had changed in ways she could never have imagined.

A few short months ago she'd been Claire, average working girl. Today she was Victoria, chosen one. Everything she learned in school, everything she had been taught at home, were mostly lies as far as she was concerned. Sure, she still clung to those deep-seated moral codes she had always lived by. Like being kind to others and having your kindness reciprocated. But codes like that did not apply to the Ones. A whole new set of internal and external rules needed to be set by Victoria.

10 months later…

She had to have a protector. She didn't want one but she knew that she *must* have one.

He waited patiently, or impatiently, she wasn't quite sure, but she recognized the controlled violence in this man. He was tall, about 6'2" she'd say, with broad shoulders and a broad chest. He looked hardened, like he had seen much, and he said little. He was handsome in his own way. Strong looking with no soft lines, hazel eyes and thick black hair and he was looking her way. He couldn't see her but she felt an unexplained energy source around him.

For some unexplained reason, Trevor wanted her to know that he felt her looking through the two-way mirror. He was intrigued by her, something he hadn't felt before. Although her face was unknown to him as of yet, something in him was being drawn to her. He would know her anywhere. She was the one. It hit him hard and he was amazed by the feeling. Feelings had long ago ceased for him. He lived hard and he knew he would die hard. This was so new to him it made him almost uncomfortable, but not quite. He quickly recovered with the anticipation of seeing this woman, knowing with certainty that coming here today changed everything.

She thought he probably benched pressed, along with some other rigorous workouts. The other men did not impress her with this specimen in the room. Although they all looked strong and cunning, he looked intelligent. His look told you he took in everything in his surroundings and was always ready for trouble.

She waited for three hours as the interviews took place. Alec and his team were in charge of the initial interviews. Waiting, her thoughts went back to the time of ignorance. It had been great. She had been unaware of the dangers of life. Oh, she knew people died every day from normal tragedies, like car accidents, and disease. But not in her wildest dreams did she suspect that there were beings here on earth not of her species. *Rather a nasty version of us,* she thought—*cunning and evil through and through.* She almost wished to be oblivious like the other souls out on the street. But she couldn't go back to being ignorant, no matter how much she wanted to.

She walked down the hall to speak with Peyton. Peyton had been a good friend these last several months. He had personally seen to it that Victoria was instructed in several languages, and brought up to speed on everything known about the Ones. Victoria had first met Peyton the day the Ones tried to attack her down at the wharf in Seattle. He had saved her and she had admired him ever since.

"Peyton, do you really believe all of this is necessary?"

"Victoria, you know it is. I know you don't want a protector but the elders have spoken. They always seem to know what is best. We need to follow their advice." The elders included Ophelia, Octavia, and Acanthus.

"I know. I know. Okay, okay enough whining. I guess I'll get back to work. Thanks, Peyton."

"Anytime. I will always be there for you if you need me."

She started to walk away but turned around, walked back a few steps and hugged Peyton. "Thank you for everything. I couldn't have held it together these last several months if not for you being there for me."

Peyton softly spoke, "You're so very welcome. It has been a privilege."

Walking down the hall, she heard Alec say, "Next!" Alec had assured her he had screened the applicants well. Although the men couldn't see her behind the mirror, they were aware someone watched them.

As the interview process proceeded she waited patiently until four men were left for her to personally interview.

She had no set questions ready, as she had decided to go with her instincts. Each man was given no specifics about her or her mission. Only that someone needed protection and it would pay well. Either way, they would be paid for their time here today.

She asked that each man be brought to her in a small room off a side hall, with only two chairs, a table, and a lamp. They would be interviewed by her and Victoria alone would decide who would be her protector. The lamp would face her guest, and away from her. She dressed in all black. Her hair was tied back in a ponytail. She had lost weight since last year, and she was a trim 125 pounds. At 5'6" it suited her. She knew she wasn't beautiful, but she had nice features with thick, lush, chestnut colored hair that occasionally turned heads.

The first man came in. He was handsome in his own right. Slim, average height, with shamefully gorgeous blonde hair, he walked in striding most confidently. He took her hand and shook it firmly.

It struck her; he probably had a way with most women. He told her his name was Nate Waters. He had served with the Navy Seals back in '08. He had a most impressive resume. He was clearly a man to rely on, the best of the best. He wanted to know more about her and her mission.

Briefly, she answered a few questions before moving on.

"I will tell you this, Mr. Waters, you will need to use all your skills and then some. There are those that seek me and would do me harm at any cost." Victoria felt an immediate rapport with this man. He was personable and capable.

"If you are indeed the selected individual, you will be briefed fully I assure you. I will inform you of my decision after all of the initial interviews are over, Mr. Waters." He had yet asked about the pay. "Mr. Waters, are you not interested in what I might be paying for your services?"

"No ma'am, if I am selected you will pay my usual fee times two without question if you want the job done, and done right." They conversed awhile longer, she thanked him for his time, and he exited the room.

Alec came in and inquired as to how things were progressing. After conferring for several minutes, he made his way down the hall to call the next interviewee in.

The second man had a stature that indicated he had lived hard, and survived by any means possible. He had visible scars on one arm and scars on the side of his face as well. To others, that may have been a source of intimidation, but to her, it bespoke of mistakes that had been made.

She politely asked some questions but it quickly became clear to her that he was getting fed up with the interview process. Almost dumping himself in the chair he huffed and let out an agitated noise somewhat like a sigh but ruder. He cut right to the chase, immediately inquiring how much was the job and when did it start. As if to say that he had more important matters to attend to. As he seated himself, silently she made her choice. She asked a few more questions, and regarded him with a healthy dose of trepidation.

Rather roughly he stated his name was Otis. He spoke of his previous missions, the men he had killed, and the woman who was a bitch. She was glad that Alec had insisted one of his men would stand guard outside the room, to be called on if necessary. After another round of questions she felt sure that he was the type of person to carry out a mission for either side, or both sides, if the right amount of cash was offered. He was all about Otis.

"I thank you for coming. You will be informed of my decision shortly. Please return to the waiting room."

He looked long and hard at her unmoving. When he finally spoke his voice was chilling, "I expect to be *informed* soon. I will need to make arrangements for my upcoming mission with you. I have decided you will be protected by me."

In that moment something came forth. It came forth from her being, something from the farthest corners, silently waiting to emerge. It was frightening yet she openly embraced it. It was a part of her that was finally awakened and it was raw power she would learn to use. It came bubbling to the surface, like dolphins corralling sardines for the kill.

Focus and determination were driving the forces. They wanted out to explore and grow. She knew with power there must be restraint and reasoning. The need for meaningful contemplation how to use this new source would be later. Right now, Mr. Otis was threatening her.

"I have decided you are unsuitable for this mission. Or any mission, for that matter, with this organization. You will take your leave now or suffer the consequences, *Mr. Otis.*"

Standing up, he leaned forward and put both his hands on the desk. He immediately retrieved his hands and starting shaking them. "Damned bitch, what did you do?" He appeared to be in considerable agony. The palm of his hands seemingly burnt.

The guard quickly opened the door. "Ma'am, do you need me?" The guard took the scene in and apprised the situation; his weapon in position. Otis was shaking his hands, attempting to ease the pain.

"Yes, be so kind as to show Mr. Otis out. Please notify Alec he needs proper payment for his services."

"Yes ma'am." With the guard behind him holding his weapon at the ready, they exited the room.

It took some time to sort things out and get back on schedule. Victoria used the short amount of time to try to come to grips with how exactly she had burnt Otis's hands. She hadn't intended to do that, but the second he put his hands menacingly on the table, she reacted immediately. The thought was instantly transformed to deed. It was as if the power within her would always attempt to protect her, with or without her permission.

Soon thereafter, the third man stepped in the room striding as though he was very confident.

"Hello, most people call me Hammer."

"Why?" she asked.

"Because I'm hard headed, I reckon."

"I see. Well, Mr. Hammer please take a seat."

As he sat down she noticed a scar running down his arm. It looked like someone or something had taken a lot of his skin. He followed her eyes and said, "I had a run in with some men who thought I was an easy kill. I proved them wrong."

"How long have you been in your current line of work, Mr. Hammer?"

"Ever since I was born to two rebels."

As she was getting ready to inquire further, he said, "Excuse me ma'am, but what exactly are you looking for here?"

"I am looking for a protector, Mr. Hammer. Someone, who can safely take me all the way to my destination."

"I am that man, Miss. I fight hard and lose never."

"I am quite sure of that Mr. Hammer. I can tell you are the type of person who stays focused on his mission. How, Mr. Hammer, would you be able to guarantee my safety?"

He viewed her as if really seeing her for the first time. "Why, I think we would get along real nice like. And, I assure you, I would take real good care of you."

She had no doubt what was going through his mind. He had no idea what kind of danger she could bring down on him.

"I wish to thank you for coming, Mr. Hammer. You will be informed of my decision shortly."

"Thank you, ma'am."

The last man, the one that had the hazel eyes entered. She realized at that moment she was holding her breath. Quickly taking a deep refreshing breath, inhaling his scent, like the crisp morning air after a light rain shower, she watched him slowly walk into the room assessing her and his surroundings. He didn't look pleased as he sat down.

"I prefer the lamp to be facing the wall," he said.

Victoria said, "Please turn it then."

He stood up and moved the direction of the lamp and renewed his assessment of her as he sat down. "What are you afraid of?"

"Many things."

He studied her for several seconds, as she did him.

"Tell me what you want."

She decided to instead ask some questions first. "May I ask your name?"

"You may ask, but I may not tell."

She waited.

He said, "My name is Trevor."

"Trevor, will you please tell me if you are trustworthy?"

He raised his eyebrows and said, "Only to those I want to be."

"I see. If the pay is right?"

"I told you, only to those I want to be."

"Hmm. Will you protect me if I pay you to, and would you take a bullet for me?"

"Can't say, I don't know you."

"Can you guarantee my safe passage all the way to my destination?"

"No."

"Tell me then, Trevor, are you a good person?"

With no hesitation, he simply said, "No."

She had known from the start he would be the one. "Well then, Trevor, I ask that you allow me to hire you with triple your normal fees. I will need to leave by Monday next. If you accept, you cannot leave this place. All your needs will be met. As you cannot guarantee my safety, I cannot guarantee yours. You will be thoroughly informed and any questions answered."

He sat quietly looking into her eyes. She said nothing and dared not look away.

"Are you running from the Ones?" he asked.

She looked questioningly into his eyes as she answered, "Yes."

"I will require full details."

"Alright."

"I also require your acceptance that I will be in charge. I command. You have to be willing to follow my orders." He saw the look of surprise on her face. He added, "Split second decisions must be made, and you must follow me without hesitation, for both of our sakes."

She digested this information and came to a decision. "I am willing to do as you request. I need an expert, Trevor, to possibly survive. I am no fool."

"Good," is all he said. He got up out of his chair and headed for the door. He stopped short of going out into the hallway. He asked without turning around, "with the answers I gave you, why did you pick me?"

"I trust next to no one Trevor, but I know in my gut that I can at least trust you to be honest with me, good or bad." He said nothing as he left the room and quietly walked down the hall.

Chapter 12

The other mercenaries were set to leave the next morning. They left with little fanfare, as their appointed destinations had already been assigned. One of the interviewees, Mr. Waters, would be considered as a possible recruit. Few made the final cut and all indications were, Mr. Waters seemed to be the complete package.

Mulling over her plans, and the ramifications thereof, Victoria moved down the hall to meet with Mr. Trevor. He walked into the room quietly. She hadn't heard any approaching footsteps. He moved with a fluid grace and his physique was sending her hormones into overdrive.

Somehow the room felt different with him in it. He had this presence about him that commanded your attention to his person. As he walked over to a chair, Victoria took in his well-defined muscular body and his dark full head of hair. She appreciated what she saw, but looked away when his eyes met hers, as she had been slowly working her way up his toned body. She felt a blush creeping its way up her face. Before she could think of anything intelligent to say, Trevor saved her the trouble.

"What is your name," he asked.

"My name is Victoria Rivers."

"Why do the Ones hunt for you?"

She looked directly into his piercing eyes, "Because I am one of them."

His calm demeanor quickly changed. He sat forward, his eyes and voice visibly hardened. "Explain."

"I have Ones blood running in me. Recently, it was discovered that my grandmother, Sylvia, was born a twin. Her brother, Jonathan, never knew of her existence. She was taken away and saved. Her identity was revealed on her deathbed. Someone very close to her has betrayed me. They now seek to get their hands on me as the sole remaining link to the human world. I must make my way to the Caves of the Forgotten, if I am to survive."

"Why would I risk all to save you?"

She knew he would ask this of her. She had to convince him or she would surely lose all. "I am three quarters human and one quarter Ones. I now have knowledge, with more coming to me every day, which could bring down the Ones. If they can convert me, I will be very dangerous for humans. This is why I chose you. I trust you to honor my wishes." She went on before he could remark, "I trust you to kill me should my capture be imminent. Your payment has already arrived to your designated offshore account. You can verify it."

"If this is so, what would stop me from tearing this place apart and retrieving my payment right now?"

"Nothing—you are free to go. The money will still be there. You have my word." She held her breath. Several seconds went by. He did not speak, nor did she. They looked into each other's eyes intensely. She felt as if she could see into his very soul, and he could see into hers. What she saw looked sound. This man would be a gentle lover, but a lethal adversary to her enemies.

She was still trying to make sense of her reaction to Trevor, when he abruptly got up from his chair and said, "Get some sleep Victoria, we have a long, hard, road ahead of us." He left, not once glancing back as Victoria watched him leave. She hoped she had made the right decision. Heaven help her if she hadn't.

Victoria lay in bed that night examining the reasons behind appointing Trevor as her protector. Ten months ago, she had been another person. The kind that kept to herself except beyond her safe number of friends that never asked too much or offered too much. She had been naïve, going about life with little direction. Oh, she had definitely, thoroughly, thought through her life goals, but they had been shallow ideas at best. The bigger picture had eluded her. And, she had merrily gone along, never questioning the tough questions of life—the hows and whys of life.

Trevor was obviously a hardened man, the type of man Claire would have stayed away from at all costs. Claire would not have been able to understand how anyone would be able to get along, let alone live with, someone like Trevor. He probably had his own set of rules, and lived by them hard and fast.

But Victoria recognized she was open to seeing Trevor in a different light. This man would stand by you. He would kill to protect those he valued. He was unlike any other man she had ever met.

Claire had been a very different person from Victoria. Claire had not had an understanding of all things evil. Things she could never have imagined that really did take place. But Claire had had one thing that Victoria would never have—an air of innocence. She could never go back to Claire.

Trevor was strong and he was venturous. He would make a good partner. Perhaps, she thought, she subconsciously longed to have some of that dangerous internal strength. That, she decided, was the reasoning behind choosing this man over the other applicants—a very logical choice indeed. Perhaps. She saw his face as she drifted off to sleep.

Chapter 13

They broke camp at daybreak. They had traveled for over six days now. They spoke only about safe issues when not speaking about the mission. Victoria knew how to play the dating game in the world she previously lived in, but now she found it difficult to act "normal."

Trevor seemed to be lost in his own thoughts today. Victoria tried to strike up a conversation.

"Trevor, what do you think about our current space program, or lack thereof?" *Ouch, this is almost as bad as asking about the weather stupid.*

"I think they need to find the planet the Ones came from and send them back."

Of course, everything came back to the Ones. The Ones could change everything. She needed to remember that.

"I'm sorry. I don't like the Ones much. They have made my life hell, and I want to send them back where they belong."

Nothing else was said for hours. She went over in

her mind all the objectives of the mission. The possible different strategies she would need to implement.

They arrived at a house in the lower part of the valley. It was small and contemporary, nestled in the tree line. She noticed a small stream on the side of the house that ran behind and down from the forest. It weaved its way through the forest floor with its gentle curves and its endless water trailing over the little pebbles and small rocks along the way. It then cut across the land with green grass on each side. The stream meandered along, separating the land, for as far as the eye could see. Some force of nature had gouged out a deep crevice in the land beyond the forest floor and then filled it with water. The stream was perfectly protected by the embankment on both sides rising up approximately fifteen feet high.

Returning to the house she saw that it was steel from the outside with windows at least two stories high. Although the exterior looked to be made of steel it was a matte material and the color of camouflage. The windows had roll down shutters of the same material. The inside was equally stunning with the entry foyer and the grand room filled with rich textures and bold colors.

The house was beautiful but that had not impressed Victoria. She was more of a garden girl.

Jackie Mae

The atrium housed all multitude of flora. It reminded her that not so long ago the people in her building used to bring their sad little plants to her, for her to revive them.

Trevor found her in the atrium. "You like plants?"

With a broad smile on her face, she said, "I love plants. I used to dream about being a master gardener when I was little. Later, when I became a teenager I wanted to have my very own gardening show. By the time I became a young adult though, with mounting bills piling up from my college years, I passed up my dream for the financial world. I learned a little too late there's no do-overs."

He came next to her. Gingerly, he put his arm around her shoulder and gave her a squeeze. "When this whole thing is over, you should get a small patch of land and work it as you can, for some peace of mind."

His insightfulness surprised her. "What do you do for some peace of mind?"

"Me? Oh, I like to mess around with Bonsai. I have maybe five or six now. Five true bonsai, six if you count the pathetic little plant I received from the son of one of my men. The little boy, Johnny, asked me to 'take care' of it for him. A couple of them are around eight years old."

"Well you are just full of surprises. That sounds like such a peaceful pastime. I would love to see your collection when we get back."

It came out before she had thought about it. Sometimes there was a disconnect between her mouth and her brain, or maybe her brain just did what it wanted before she could talk herself out of it; before her reasoning stepped in—the reasoning that always analyzed and found a reason not to do something. There was always a reason lurking nearby it seemed. It was one of the reasons among many that she had not fully embraced in her life up until now.

He looked pleased. "Yes, it would please me to share my bonsai with you. Very few people have ever seen them; it seems we have something in common."

Somehow, in the space of mere seconds, the atmosphere changed. There were electrical charges pinging around the room. At the center stood Trevor, and he was gazing into her eyes, waiting. Hunger, sheer sexual hunger, was clinging to him. A surge of awareness in Victoria awakened long lost feelings of need.

Scared of her feelings, afraid to take a leap of faith, she stood her ground. Her heart insisted she close the gap and wrap her arms around Trevor's neck and kiss him thoroughly, but her reasoning told her to stand her ground and think long and hard about the ramifications. There were a million zillion reasons standing in her way. Fighting through the tangled web of reasons, she crossed the room until she was standing directly in front of Trevor.

His smile was her undoing. She rose up on her toes and wrapped her arms around his neck. He bent his head down and kissed her. It was pure, like the rushing spring water running down the mountain side after a long winter's melt. Her senses were taking her to a place she never traveled to before. The exquisite care with which he touched her cheek, framing her face with his hands, left her breathless with anticipation, hope, longing, all wrapped up together. It was magical.

She was unable to form a coherent thought. That's why she didn't see the change in Trevor's face at first. He moved out of her arms and headed toward the monitors. "What's wrong Trevor?"

"We have company coming." His demeanor changed; he looked hardened, battle ready.

Thoughts were racing through her mind. Should she reveal her secrets to Trevor? Was he in it for the long haul? Where did he fit in with the rebellion, with her?

"What do you want me to do?"

Position yourself away from windows and in front of the monitors. I need to check on something. Scream if you see the Ones approaching."

"I need to tell you something—something crucial. You have to understand, I was going to tell you before we reached the Forgotten Caves."

He stopped in his tracks, "Tell me." He sounded quietly furious. His look said it all. This wasn't good.

"My grandmother was born with a twin brother. I'm the chosen one."

"Dammit. Why didn't you tell me?" He held up his hand when she started to speak. "No, there's no time for this right now, but you have to answer for this Victoria. I want the full story."

"Yes."

He left the room then. She focused on the monitors. All at once on the far monitor she detected movement. The foliage was immense but there had been something out of place.

"Trevor," she screamed.

"Yes."

"Back perimeter."

"Got it." He disappeared again for a few minutes, reappearing with several devices.

With no time to ask further questions, she listened as he gave instructions.

"You can push this mechanism to activate all the nasty surprises set up. This one is for the front perimeter and this one is for the back. If you see the Ones in either location use it."

Trevor started to walk away. "Wait. Where are you going?" screamed Victoria.

"I have to secure some things," answered Trevor.

He had said it in a way that implied she didn't need to know at that moment, which seriously irritated Victoria.

"Fine."

Her set face let him know he might be mad about her not telling him everything but she felt she had had good reasons. He walked then but she refused to feel guilty.

Everything was quiet for about ten minutes. It was then the Ones came at the house with a force of energy. She couldn't see anything but she felt a stirring in her mind, like they were looking for her, probing the atmosphere around her. It was unsettling to feel it. It was like the goose bumps you get right before the monster finds the victim and eats him in the movies.

Trevor came into the room, "Here." He motioned for her to give him the triggers which she gladly did. Her head was beginning to hurt. She backed up slightly as he pushed them. Immediately a scream could be heard.

"That's right you bastards," exclaimed Trevor. The high was short lived as three or four Ones beat at the defenses. Within five minutes it was apparent whatever they were using to break through was going to work.

"Listen, Victoria, I want you to follow what I say. The Ones will be in shortly and you have to do what I say, when I say it."

Victoria calmly walked over to where an extra gun lay on the table. Retrieving it, she looked down at it long and hard, walking back over to where Trevor stood watching as she handed it to him.

"I cannot allow the Ones to get their hands on me. I am not strong enough against them yet. I will not let that happen. The rebellion depends on me not becoming like those abominations. You have to shoot me." She took several steps back facing him.

"I am not, repeat, I am not going to shoot you."

There was an invader. It was just out of reach but it was searching for her. The pressure in her head was becoming unbearable.

"Now. You must do it now."

"No Victoria."

"I trusted you! I trusted you," screamed Victoria. "Please, please do it now. I can't become a Ones. Please, if you can't, I can, just give me the damn gun!"

"Victoria. Please, you have to trust me."

"Why should I?" she roared.

"You know I didn't know the whole story, Victoria. I didn't know you were the chosen one. Stay with me. Please. Please stay, and give me your trust."

Critical seconds went by. Seconds she didn't have. She looked into his eyes. It was there in his eyes; his determination, his strength, his integrity.

"Yes, I will give you my trust. But know this; I didn't give it to anyone else. No one else."

"I understand," is all he said. All he had time to say.

They burst into the room and wave after wave of evil swamped all her senses. She felt sluggish, and looked for Trevor. Although they wanted her, they seemed not to care about Trevor; he was being tortured by some means that she couldn't fathom. He was fighting some unseen force and was holding his head in his hands, as if that would somehow drive out the demons.

It was all surreal, and time moved in slow motion. Her brain couldn't process it all. In what seemed a lifetime of torture for Trevor, he moved swiftly in a heartbeat, and the surprised Ones took a tentative step back. Trevor paid no attention to her. He kept his eyes focused on the Ones. He made a slow small smile that would have made her run like hell on wheels if he were looking her way. Instead, the Ones looked both uneasy and unsure. Palm out, he turned that unseen force on the Ones, and they screamed with agony. She stared at him in open-mouthed astonishment. They retreated out the door, and moved so fast they were gone in a flash.

She looked at Trevor as she started to fall. He moved unbelievably fast and was there holding her before she hit the ground. He spoke softly. He told her that they would be fine, that he would protect her. Her head and muscles were screaming silently from the onslaught, and she felt faint.

"I—I just need a moment. Sorry."

He eased her down to the ground where they sat together. He looked out the window in the direction the Ones had fled.

"We need to leave this place now—right now."

She forced herself to stir. Giving no more thought to the pain coursing through her body, she moved with renewed determination beside Trevor. Life depended on it.

How had Trevor fought against the Ones? Who was he really? Victoria had so many questions that needed answers, but she was running for her life, and she had a headache from hell.

They had been gone for days now and she had naïvely thought they would make it to the Forgotten Caves without running into any Ones. It turned out to be a foolish thought. Somehow many of the answers to her destiny were to be revealed in the caves. Her powers were to be increased there as well. So, she really had no choice but to make the trek across this land to try to reach it in secrecy.

Traveling for hours now in silence, Trevor gestured for her to rest. No argument whatsoever as she thankfully lowered her exhausted body down to the ground. It felt wonderful. If she had not been so exhausted she would have appreciated the beauty of her surroundings more. They had stopped near a lake that appeared to be several miles wide and the whole area was teeming with wildlife. She had already observed deer, fox, and even a stray raccoon. That meant there were probably lots of mountain lions as well. She was not the least bit afraid of that awesome predator because she now knew who the real scary monsters were.

She rested her eyes as she leaned back against a tree. She watched Trevor put one of his many knives down on the ground. After a minute or two she saw him get up, walk behind a stand of trees near a big boulder, presumably to relieve himself. She eyed the knife; she needed to have something should it be necessary to take action herself, she contemplated. But the sheer exhaustion was taking its toll; she would just rest one or two more seconds and then she would…

"Jonathon is waiting for you," whispered a voice. "Go to the forest edge, right now, Victoria. He will be waiting. Jonathon is waiting for you Victoria." She heard it repeated over and over in her mind.

She woke up with a start. Trevor was still there, not gone. It all came back to her in a rush. The horror and the shame that she had not helped Trevor fight the Ones laid over her like a heavy suit of armor.

Trevor looked her way. "It's not your fault; they were holding you prisoner with their control."

"I should have done more," she said looking down at the ground. She needed to change the subject.

"Trevor, the Ones visited my dreams. They told me to go to the forest edge, and wait for Jonathon."

"That can only mean we are beginning to worry the Ones. Victoria, I need to teach you how to defend yourself."

"You need to answer some questions first."

He waited a heartbeat and said, "Come here, Victoria, please."

She came with no hesitation. He held her in his arms and brushed her hair back. He looked at her and she felt like she would very much like to look into his eyes forever. But, of course, she knew he detested the Ones, and she was one of them. He was only being tolerant. *A man like him, would never like a woman like me, not in the way that counts,* she thought. She was the lowest of the low in his eyes, and she had practically thrown herself at him earlier.

He shifted his body to come closer. She was suddenly breathless; anticipation soared through her body, leaving all thoughts that this was not a good idea far behind. He pushed her up close, so that she could feel his power, his need. He slowly lowered his head, all the while looking intently at her, giving her time to refuse. Her only coherent thoughts revolved around the heat of his body that engulfed her, and made her feel deliciously wonderful. She was dazed and euphoric at the same time. He had cast a spell over her. She could not, would not, refuse. She wanted this.

He kissed her so that she felt the earth and sky move around her. She was sinking into a field of flowers with only sunshine all around her. When he gently, reluctantly, ended the kiss, she needed to lean into him for support. Her knees felt weak and at the same time she felt wonderfully empowered with a new sense of self. He had somehow changed her forever, with that one kiss.

"We need to strengthen your ability to push back at the Ones. But not too hard; we don't want them to know your true powers."

"Power, what power?" She struggled to focus. "I was putty in their hands."

"Victoria, you have powers you have yet to explore."

She turned this new information over in her mind. She had felt a twinge of power waiting in the wings, when the Ones had attacked her—and again, when they whispered in her dream, but she didn't have any idea how to tap into it.

"How do you know these things? Tell me, Trevor—the whole truth here, if you please."

"You are not the only one born from a set of twins, Victoria."

She could only gape at him. "You are part Ones as well?"

"Yes, I am one quarter Ones like you," answered Trevor.

"My god, why didn't you tell me?" she screamed.

"I wasn't sure at first if you were the real deal, or just another plant from the Ones. I had to be sure, dammit." He had known it would not go over good when he finally told her the truth.

She walked away. How could she have been so stupid? She had trusted him. She had never trusted anyone since she had found the truth; no one except Trevor, that is. He was just like the rest. She needed to get out of here. Somehow get word to a handler. She definitely needed a new protector. But who could she trust?

She moved toward the door.

"No, you don't Victoria."

"Yes, I can," she stated. "Your damn money is available as you requested. Leave me alone. I am going my own way and you can't stop me."

"I not only can, I will," said Trevor with conviction.

She stood there reeling in anger, full of rage. She knew by the look in his eyes he meant it, but she just didn't understand why. She stomped her foot hard enough to cause pain on the morrow.

"You have your money, the mission is over. Let me pass."

"You aren't going anywhere until I make you understand."

"Oh, I understand alright, perfectly."

"Sit down Victoria, you're mad, hurt, and not thinking straight."

She wanted to scream, to hurt him. She had to leave this place. Leave the Ones behind. Go back to Claire. But she couldn't. She just couldn't.

Her mind melting moment was over, and she knew she had to be strong. She could use this man as well. He had his agenda and she had hers. They could trust each other enough to get things done. She would not make the mistake to trust more than that.

"I'm fine now, *Mr.* Trevor. Show me what I need to learn."

"Not now, Victoria, I think we need to get to a safe haven to lick our wounds. I will be sick very soon, and I will need your strength to get me there."

She looked to him with concern. She immediately said, "What? Where are you hurt?" *God, I'm so stupid.* "Sit down, let me look you over."

"No, Victoria, they are on our trail, not far behind. They follow our prints."

She didn't understand what he meant by prints, but decided to let it go for now. "Move out," she said instead.

They went several miles without talking. Engrossed in her thoughts for quite a while, she slowly began to notice subtle changes in his breathing; sweat started to break out over his brow, and he was definitely slowing his pace.

Finally, he said, "I need to sit down."

"Tell me now, Trevor, what is going on? What is wrong with you? How far are we from a safe place ahead? If you need me, you will have to trust me too."

That stung by the look on his face, but fair. "I'm sorry, sorrier than you would believe," he stated. "The Ones injected a pulsating poison into my head that will disable me for several hours very soon. They know this and are racing to find us. They will stop at nothing to get to us. Taking you, with your inexperience to fight them, is going to be easy in their eyes. We will use this to our advantage. I am going to show you what to do. You will have to be strong."

What else could go wrong, she thought.

After a couple more grueling hours, they stopped. Victoria didn't see anything that looked like a shelter until Trevor moved several bushes to one side.

"After you, my lady."

Victoria gazed at the interior; it looked to be an opening about five feet high and approximately five or six feet in width. She immediately hunched over and advanced. After about only ten to twelve feet she was able to stand up. It was pitch black. As soon as Trevor joined her he turned on a light and shone it around the cave. It was surprisingly big, gigantic even. One would never have thought this was right there in the middle of the forest. Strikingly beautiful in its own way, Victoria took her time taking it all in.

"Amazing isn't it?"

"Unique to say the least," she replied. She was already getting a little chilled in here. She shivered.

He led her to another tunnel that led to another, much smaller room. This room provided a little warmth.

"Are you still cold? We could move to the next room if you wish?"

"No." She sat down ending the discussion.

He was trying to create small talk. Victoria would have none of it. She was still feeling betrayed—although, if she were in the mood to be fair, she probably would have done the same thing. But she wasn't in the mood to be fair. He had hurt her. Hurt her in a way she thought she was immune to.

With all the upheaval in her life this last year, she thought she had safely stored away her deepest feelings. This man was affecting her, and she didn't like it. She needed to keep this impersonal. Lying would do no good, for she knew she was well on her way of being too far gone to keep it merely impersonal anymore. He was becoming very personal to her and she wondered just how he might be feeling. Not that she had time for this. She was in the middle of a mission, and she needed to get a grip. One kiss was one kiss. And, she was sure he must have seen it that way as well.

"Victoria, do you want me to start?"

She had been so engrossed in her own world of thoughts. She scolded herself for forgetting her priorities, her duty. "Yes, I'm ready." *Focus Victoria— there are more important matters right now.*

"Okay. I have already witnessed your ability to push your power somewhat. I can sense it in you. You are stronger than you think. And, I suspect you will come into more gifts as you get stronger too. I need to teach you some simple maneuvers to shield yourself, should you have the need. I will also show how to hurl some of your powers and how to hide your presence for a short duration."

"Wow, I can do all that?"

"And so much more, Victoria."

Two hours later, Trevor looked totally exhausted. He had painstakingly showed her how to apply her powers a little and how to defend herself as well. She had learned so much in so little time. Her knowledge was naturally growing each day and with Trevor teaching her she was sure she would be able to make a difference. Looking over at Trevor it was clear he was waning and was now finding it hard to stay awake.

Chapter 14

She moved about the cave entrance restlessly. She had done all she could, she assured herself. Trevor was resting at last. He had argued with her when she strongly suggested he go to sleep. He had resisted until she used the information he himself had provided earlier.

"Victoria, I will stay awake to help guide you as you fight the Ones. I will, however, pay for it."

How?" she questioned him.

The deep sleep will replenish my reserves and I will be at full power within a few hours' time, but fighting it will be painful and will lengthen the amount of time required to heal."

So, Victoria had convinced him to sleep the deep sleep because she was sure that their plan would work. She would need him to be at full power for what lay ahead.

She was not so confident now. What if she had been wrong? What if she couldn't follow through with the plan? So many negative thoughts were flying in her head; she had to mentally close that door. She had to think clearly now and stay focused on the task at hand, no matter that she was truly alone. She had to do this. She had to be successful. No one might ever know who Victoria was, but she couldn't think of that now. This was too important to screw up.

Trevor needed her to protect him; she would do her best. She walked back through the maze of tunnels. Seeing Trevor laying there wounded, his body so still he looked as if dead, made her contemplate what sacrifices may lay ahead. Trevor had taught her a simply protection layer she could apply if she found herself in need. She decided she needed to know there would be added protection over Trevor. She followed his teachings and felt the atmosphere in the cave change. Satisfied, she walked away and forced herself not to look back.

She walked five miles back to help ensure the Ones wouldn't be able to find Trevor should she fail. She had taken the weapon that Trevor had insisted she take but she had never used a weapon against anyone before and she wasn't sure she could use it. Even with her recent training she knew it was one thing to prepare, but another issue altogether actually to use it. By nature, Victoria was a very compassionate person. Her entire life she had been helpful and kind. This new person she was being forced to embody; this new, much harder, state of being was most difficult for Victoria to accept. Getting stronger of mind and body, she would be forced to accept her newfound person.

This plan had to work. Hopefully, she would be back at the cave soon and she would watch over Trevor as long as he needed to sleep. They weren't that far from their destination and many things would become clearer once they arrived.

Chapter 15

She heard or felt the Ones approaching, she wasn't sure which. Whispering through the trees, as gentle as rain, she heard her name called on the breeze. An insistent push told her they had started their assault. Trevor had assured her they needed her alive. She was banking on that.

She stood still as they approached. There were three of them, spread apart coming toward her slowly. They stopped midway, assessing her. They each had full length robes on, with hoods covering their heads. She pulled her weapon out, but before she could even raise it up, something hit her hand and the weapon was thrown approximately ten feet away. Ignoring her painful hand she kept her eyes on the Ones. They raised their arms and started to weave a pattern in the air. Trevor had warned her they would do this. She said the words, "No one is safe, no one is home, and the weavers hands are made of stone." She projected her voice, using a weaving pattern of her own.

The Ones were stunned. Their hands began to harden and weigh them down. As they were forced to lower themselves, they said a series of words that alleviated almost immediately, the damage to their hands. They renewed their forward motion and looked to her intently with new determination.

Even though she felt more scared than at any other time in her life, she showed no signs of terror. She too, moved forward. She decided now was the time to take out the one on the left for he looked like the leader. The Ones had looked to him twice already, as if asking for permission. She shifted seamlessly toward the left, and pushed with all her power. He fell instantly. A look of shock and rage spread upon his face. He extended his arm out and blasted Victoria with a pulsating beat that she was sure would disable her, or, probably would kill her. She fell against a bush and tried to right herself so she could rise, but the two Ones were on her in an instant. They grabbed her, and jerked her up. They were going to inject her; she saw the syringe.

Something in her snapped. She projected a mind numbing scream in the minds of the Ones with such intensity that the syringe fell to the ground and the Ones themselves had no ability to fight her—they writhed in pain.

Contrary to her upbringing, Victoria had no problem wiping these Ones off the map at this moment in time. They were responsible for her parent's deaths—the destruction of her home, her life. They were evil and justice needed to be meted out.

Before she could formulate a plan, and the rightness of it, the supposed ring leader threw a metal object toward her. It pierced her arm with such intensity that she had to scream from the pain. She could feel a numbing sensation that was threatening to cause a blackout.

She blocked the pain, and looked directly at the one who threw the object, for he was now smiling an evil smile and moving forward yet again. Victoria hurled the object back. She never touched it. It was moved with her mind. Not questioning how she had managed that feat, she pushed it with all her might. It imploded on impact inside the one who had hurt her. He, along with the other Ones perished and all that was left was red dust that swiftly blew away.

She lowered herself to the ground, as the pain intensified. She knew she should check on Trevor. That was the last thought she had as she closed her eyes.

Chapter 16

Trevor became aware that morning had arrived. He realized Victoria should have been back by now. He moved swiftly off the makeshift bed with a lethal quality only a hardened man like himself could accomplish. Even though he had just awoken from a disabling form of poison, he ran to the spot that Victoria had last been, determined they had drugged her, and carried her off. He cursed. He wasted no time with regrets—that way was useless. Now he had to locate Victoria, and retrieve her no matter what the cost.

He made his way to the base of the mountain chain. Hours later, having had a joint meeting with his men, he made his decision.

He made the call.

Fundor, the destroyer, had given him the coordinates. He knew they would have tracked him, and they would bring forces. They now needed him as well. He had successfully hidden his secret until now from the Ones. He knew the moment he had turned the tables on the Ones, the game would be up. He'd had no choice.

He could not allow them to have her, as she was his. He had known the moment he laid eyes on her, she was his destiny. But she could never know. The seer had told him he would not live long, that he would perish fighting Fundor. Normally, he would not have given any credit to the notion, except be it that this seer was none other than his great uncle on his mother's side. Salmun, the seer, said his death would be noble. Trevor could not imagine his death as being noble. Salmun had also indicated he would save the life of a most important one. He intended to do just that. He clung to that prediction.

The full moon was on the horizon. The Ones were hiding amongst the brush and rock formations. They were like vermin. Their minions hid in plain sight amongst the ordinary hard working folks across the earth. He loathed them, and had looked forward to the day when he would wipe them off the map. But now, he had more important things to accomplish. He wanted to see Victoria released and unharmed, one last time. He hoped she would live a healthy, long life of happiness.

Quan and Visor appeared to his left ending his roaming thoughts.

"Trevor, are you ready, sir?"

"Yes Visor, move into position."

The small force had assembled and moved with determination toward their goal. Their mission was to capture Fundor and kill as many of the Ones as possible. He hoped to learn the location of Victoria. The snipers lay in wait; they were fast and lethal in any given situation. Trevor trusted his men explicitly.

Fundor would try to acquire him as soon as he could, and he knew why. They would require Trevor to lure Victoria into the initiation. Once she had agreed, there would be no turning back. And the Ones would rule the world. Mankind would be used to further their cause.

Quan used telepathy to tell Trevor the Ones were approaching from the northeast; a lone rider was advancing. The lone rider came close to the outcropping above the stream and halted. Quan signaled it was a go. Trevor knew this was the best opportunity for them to make a try for him.

Trevor moved to the location gestured by the rider, and waited. He silently said to one and all, that he would not fail; he *would* find Victoria—his Victoria.

He did not have to wait long. The fight was fierce. The clashes and screams served as proof that death rained down on them. Two Ones threw their diejons straight into the chest of one of his men. Trevor rammed into them knocking both Ones to the ground. Trevor raised his knife in an arch, swiftly slicing cleanly through both Ones' throats. Knowing that they were good and dead, he wasted no time, moving on to his next victim. In the end, riders and foot soldiers lay strewn about like some sort of domino effect.

The stench was already becoming prevalent, but Trevor knew there was one hiding amongst the dead. He closed his eyes to truly see. He opened his eyes and knelt beside a seemingly fallen soldier. He put his knee on the woman and smashed her head back against the ground as she tried to launch her weapon. He threw it aside and forced the enemy to sit up. He manipulated her arms behind her back, and tied them together. She spat on the ground but refused to show any signs of pain. He knew questioning her would be useless. She knew nothing,

He reacted just in the nick of time, as another fallen soldier that Trevor had not noticed leveled his weapon in the direction of Trevor's chest. His quick reaction time saved his life, but did not save him from the gaping wound that was now etched on his arm. He did not have time to gauge how much blood was running down his arm, as the soldier lunged for him. The pain threatened to slow him down. He shoved the female in front and to the side of him. As he came to his feet, he removed his stars from his buckle and sent them flying into the chest wall of the man lunging himself toward him. He fell at Trevor's feet with his eyes wide open and shock plainly on his face. Trevor forced the female soldier down and asked the dying man to tell him where Fundor was. The man tried to form words, but blood was trickling from his mouth.

Trevor leaned down to better hear the dying man say, "You will initiate Victoria, and Fundor will rule the world. Submit or suffer the consequences." He coughed up some blood as Trevor attempted to secure the whereabouts of Fundor one last time.

"Your passing will not be in vain if you help me find Victoria."

The dying man looked into Trevor's eyes and just stared. The dying man spoke when Trevor was sure there would be no more. "Fundor can be found at the base of the Truid Mountains, in the area known as, The Darkest Hour." Those were his last words in this life.

The woman cursed at him in her native language and Trevor reacted by punching her jaw. She said no more and sat stoically.

"Are you alright, sir?" Nash moved over to him. He looked down at his injured arm.

"Yes."

He stood up, went to see about his other men not caring of his arm.

After what seemed like hours, Trevor surveyed the land. Bloodstains dotted the landscape. The parched land seemed to soak up the blood so fast that Trevor reasoned soon no one would be able to detect what had taken place here. The bodies had already been disposed of, the prisoner removed to a safe location for interrogation.

Nash, one of his snipers, stitched up his arm. "You should live, sir." He was putting the final stitch in. He tied off the stitch as he remarked that Fundor had not been among the dead. That could only mean he had retreated along with the rest. He would always ensure his safety first. Fundor was smart, but so was Trevor.

Trevor was tracking the vermin now. His men, stalwarts, were the best of the best. They had been with him for a long time now, and were both loyal and well off because of it. They took jobs that no one else would, or could. They went to the farthest corners of the globe, and took out as many of the Ones along the way as possible.

He knew it was only a matter of time until his luck would run out. Skirting death for many years now, he had been content with life up to this point. He now knew other, bigger, and better things, existed out there. He never considered for a moment that there might be a life other than hunting and killing the Ones. Now he wanted more—so much more. And all those wants revolved around Victoria. He would find her.

Chapter 17

Victoria awoke to strange surroundings. As she was trying to clear her head, a voice from behind spoke.

"How are you feeling, Victoria?" said a strange voice from behind.

She turned her head sharply and winced as she immediately felt pain.

"Take it easy, we wouldn't want to slow down your healing process." He moved around to the front where she could better see him. He appeared to be a mixture of several ethnicities.

"Who are you, and where am I?" She struggled to sit up but found it necessary to stay down.

"I am called Vincent, and you are some place safe for the time being." He rose. "I will leave you now. You need to rest."

He closed the tall wooden door that opened into a darkened hallway. It looked ancient. She looked around and discovered a window on the far wall that had bars on it. She slowly sat up. When she knew she could stand without falling, she slowly walked over to the window.

What she saw made her gasp: a cavern of unspeakable beauty that went as far as the eye could see. The walls of the cavern were ten stories high. Every nook and cranny held some form of life. Be it ferns, or moss, or some other plant life she had never seen, it all formed a painting that you could look at infinitely.

Far below, lay a winding stream with magnificent green grass growing on both sides of the bank. It was breathtaking. She stood looking at it, basking in it all, when it dawned on her that there didn't seem to be any creatures of any kind anywhere. No bugs, no lizards, no birds, no nothing.

She closed her eyes and looked with her other vision. She opened her mind to the truth. As she opened her eyes a different sight lay before her. Filth oozed from the bars on the window. The view outside was horrid. Death and destruction lay all around. The grotto walls were barren and dismal. Animal bones lay far below, and were scattered in the darkened waters.

Her knees buckled and she fell to the dirt floor. She glanced over to the corner where she detected movement. A single mouse cowered in the corner, staring at her with its beady eyes. When it felt brave enough, it scurried away through a tiny hole in the wall.

Just as she wished she too could scurry away and leave this place behind her, and reunite with Trevor, the door opened to reveal a man that was quite tall. He had on a long flowing gown. He had long white hair, with a face that reminded her of a kindly grandfather type. The words he spoke were not that of a kindly grandfather, concerned after her health, but, rather, someone who would be vicious.

"Get up now, you will rise, Victoria, and come with me."

"What do you want?" replied Victoria.

"You know what I want, now don't you?" He cocked his head sideways, raising the ends of his lips to form a grin. An involuntary shiver coursed through her body and invoked a strong need to run.

"Who are you?"

"I am your father."

"My father is dead. I will hear no more of your lies. And, I repeat, I will not give you what you seek." Even to her ears it sounded desperate.

He just waited and gestured for her to follow. Then his serene look turned to an evil one as he said, "you may follow me now or suffer the consequences, my dear."

"You will not bend my will or determination." Victoria braced herself for the pain she knew would come. Instead, she heard a scream from far away. She searched his face and saw the satisfaction in his eyes.

"I will try again. You *will* follow me, my dear, right now."

Victoria didn't move and didn't blink. He stared at her, looking into her somehow. She felt a stirring in her mind—an intrusion. She needed to examine this newest development as soon as possible; she would figure it out before he was able to fully enter her mind, perhaps taking away her will.

"Trevor will be heartsick and hurting quite horribly, if you choose poorly."

She moved. He smiled. She followed him down the darkened stairs, lit only by dim lights cast upon the wall, that didn't quite reach the floor. She stumbled twice, and had to use her hands to keep from falling. It was a winding stone staircase that went down several flights.

They finally reached a destination. It had a massive wooden door that was arched, reminiscent of those old castle doors in all the horror movies she had watched growing up. He opened the door. The room had table after table with gadgets on them. They seemed high tech, even though her surroundings looked old and tired. She didn't have time to dwell on it because she saw Trevor sitting at one of the tables. He sat motionless. His eyes revealed nothing, and he did not speak.

It was not Trevor—another trick. Victoria closed her eyes and saw with her new, other vision. She opened her eyes. She saw before her a hideous being of small stature. *Nothing like Trevor*, she thought.

"Amazing—your powers astound me, my dear."

"I will never be your *dear* anything," she replied.

"We shall see," is all he said. He gestured for her to follow.

She had to formulate a plan, and fast before they were able to assert their will on her. She knew she was strong, but not nearly as strong as this man before her. This man more or less glided across the floor with the fluid grace of a gazelle. She sensed, rather than saw, his aura. It was pure evil. There would be no mercy from this Ones.

Moving on, they entered a room where a laboratory was in full swing. Several men and women actively worked on projects throughout the vast expanse. The 'room' was the size of a football practice field.

"This is a small sample of my brilliance. When you have taken your proper place among my people you will quickly learn to follow in my footsteps. You will glorify my existence and honor my rightful place as leader of this pitiful, puny world." He looked to her then, assessing her. "Furthermore, you will be rewarded as I see fit. I will give you a position of power under me."

Saying nothing she took her time looking around. A man in his fifties approached. He appeared to be of African descent, with black hair, probably around 180 lbs., and over 6 feet tall. He had a distinct accent, definitely African, but one she couldn't readily identify; his country of origin unknown.

"This is Dr. Diop, a physicist. He is working on something the humans worked on centuries ago: alchemy."

"Yes sir. It is my pleasure to see you today." He bowed slightly with a smile on his face and offered nothing more.

"That is all." A dismissal. Hastily, Dr. Diop took his leave backing away while bowing slightly but repeatedly.

As they walked past numerous work areas, she took note of several black canisters sitting on desktops. As they walked by the scientists, techs, whatever they were called, they all made a point to be busy looking downward.

"Come this way." He gestured with his hand. They left the white sterile environment and headed toward a door that looked ancient.

Chapter 18

She followed him back out into the hallway. It was dark and dingy. No sounds except for her own. The man made no sound as he walked. Moving to the stairs, they went down several more flights. This time he walked past many doors that all looked the same. He stopped at a door further down the hall. He motioned with his hand for Victoria to enter.

"You first," Victoria said, when it was apparent he did not intend to touch the door.

She felt a steady push toward the door, and she had to force herself down, in order to stop her forward progress. To her utter surprise, he walked up to her, lifted her up by the neck with one hand, and set her on her feet. She could not speak, for her throat was constricted and throbbing in pain. He opened the door with a silent command, and she was shoved by an unseen force into the room.

She was plunged into total darkness as the door closed. She stayed stationary and silent. As her eyes adjusted she found there was a very low level of light emitting from the floor. For several moments, she closed her eyes and saw the truth with her other vision. It was not unlike the other rooms she had visited thus far, but this room had occupants—five to be exact, two women and three soldiers, all chained to the wall. She examined each in turn. They spoke not a word, for fear was surrounding them.

"I am called Victoria. Who are you?"

The man farthest from her position hoarsely said, "I am called Trayvon. Why are you not being chained to the wall?"

Victoria was wary. "I became a prisoner today. They are testing me in some way, I imagine."

The blonde woman at the far end cried softly. "Please, if you know a way to get us out of here, help us." She was so emotional that her voice raised several pitches higher and she spoke at a rapid rate. "Help us, please. I'm pregnant and so afraid—so very afraid," she shrieked.

"Hush woman. I told you not to tell anyone that. We don't know her. She's probably one of them. She just wants to torture us some more."

The man beside the blonde woman definitely looked like he had taken the worst of the torture. His face was a mixture of blood and pus. His nose was clearly broken, one finger appeared dislocated and his eyes were swollen.

"I am with the rebellion," said Victoria. A collective sigh rang out from the prisoners.

The man that was chained beside the blonde said, "My name is Roberto. We have been here for six days now. We are starving and tired. They force us to stay awake, and beat us when we fall asleep. How did you come to this place?"

"I don't know actually. They drugged me, and I woke up in this cavern. Where are you from? How did you come to this place?"

Roberto spoke up. "We came from just south of Albuquerque. Me and the boys here, we are recent recruits. Been with the rebellion for about a month now. We were waiting for transport and decided to catch a bite to eat at Dina's Hamburger Delight. Nobody else was in the joint, just these girls here and they worked behind the counter."

"I just want to go home," wailed the blonde woman. Her tone of voice had a pitiful ring to it. She was horrified by what she had experienced thus far. Working at Dina's Hamburger Delight had not prepared her for meeting up with the Ones.

Roberto continued, "They came in disguised, so we didn't know they were the Ones. Before we knew what was happening, they had grabbed us all, and here we are." He spread his fingers as wide as possible to encompass their surroundings.

The door opened and two guards emerged with trays of food. All the lights came fully on and the chains fell away from the prisoners. They froze in place, too terrified to approach the food.

"Eat. It is not poisoned. It is a gift from our father, to honor our guest, Victoria," declared one of the guards. With that said, they scuttled out of the room and locked the door.

The group appeared hesitant and leery. She couldn't blame them, but she didn't have time to try and smooth things out. "Either you decide right here, right now to help me, or we are on opposite sides."

They all looked to her; a few looked undecided, fearful, and hopeful, while she stood her ground waiting for a decision.

A soldier that had yet to speak said, "I am called Abbott, ma'am. We need a plan. They didn't let us go to feed us. They'll expect us to try to break out." She noticed then that he was an amputee.

"That is why we will accommodate their wishes with haste."

They talked about the interior space and pathways out. Trayvon had paid close attention to his captors during his detainment. As they had taken the captives from room to room, he had used his somewhat photographic memory and had mapped out an escape route in his mind.

She explained her plan in detail. "I will hold a projection, while simultaneously holding back as many of the Ones as possible. As you know the way out, move quickly and dispatch any Ones you meet. When you reach the rise nearest the mountain chain you will find the contact." She told the men how to find him. "Tell him the coordinates of my location and tell him all necessary details to mount a rescue."

"It will be done," answered each man in turn.

She refrained from saying that she had never done anything even remotely like it before, but she felt power within her. Somehow, someway she just *knew* she could and would.

An hour later they started the keening. The chant caught the attention of the guards. As they opened the door, the guards saw the prisoners sitting in a circle. They exchanged bewildered looks and started to back away. Victoria waited patiently for the guards to back up fully before she struck the blow, which thankfully, rendered them unconscious.

As more guards were sure to respond, they quickly moved down the hall toward the exit Trayvon had logged in his memory. Victoria continued to render her presence among the prisoners as they moved down and out of the cavern. Trayvon and Abbott had successfully neutralized three more guards as they moved toward freedom. Victoria struck several guards with the full force of her mind.

When she knew with certainty they had made it out safely, she reached for Trayvon in her mind, told him that she wished him well and thanked him in advance for conveying the coordinates to those searching for her.

Trayvon was taken aback. He heard her voice clearly even though they were now miles away. He sensed that Victoria was very strong, knew she must be an invaluable leader, but nonetheless was surprised when she contacted him telepathically. Although sensitive to his surroundings and capable to sometimes act on his intuition, he had never heard voices from far away. It was awesome.

Victoria knew they would be coming for her. With certainty she knew that the women and soldiers would not have made it out if she had not aided their escape. She knew she could do this.

At first, she didn't feel it coming. Like a slimy slug, it slowly moved in her mind. Roaring at the end like an oncoming train, the steady beat disoriented her. She rallied at the last second, realizing she needed to protect herself, but it was far too late. She screamed. Her scream echoed throughout the chamber, a scream that was both bloodcurdling and horrid. The scream went on and on but no one could hear her.

Chapter 19

Trevor had tracked them to this place. They would be aware that Trevor was there and waiting. As Trevor waited, he went over his strategy yet again. All at once, a fog appeared. Creeping low to the ground, like an insidious creature devouring all within its grasp, it slowly moved toward them. He looked to Visor and indicated he should engage the patterned sequence.

Fundor had sent many of his henchmen in his place. He would hang back until it was safe, now that he knew Trevor was a dangerous opponent. The Ones attacked with viciousness.

The fog took out three men before they could manipulate the seeker. The seeker controlled the henchmen. Not the leaders, just the expendables. Using his learned ways, Trevor struck hard and fast. The Ones did not know the extent of his abilities as of yet, and therefore, did not expect him to tone down the white noise. The white noise enabled the Ones to communicate clearly with each other and empowered them somehow.

The predator was now the prey. He lashed out with his knife just as the Ones approached and attempted to hurl a diejon, a weapon of alien origins, straight at him. The diejon was a small oval shaped object that could level a pulsing chatter that would vibrate throughout your body until all control facilities would be disabled. Then the Ones could easily take over their prey. But Trevor and his men had long since figured out a way around this device; they just weren't aware of it yet.

Trevor preferred to use his knife in a fight like this. His knife cut fast and deadly. When needed, he threw the knives with precision. Always with three knives located on his person, he only removed them for showering as a rule. All his men were walking arsenals as well.

Trevor moved in and attacked the closest Ones. As they struggled, Trevor was forced to give up his position. This abomination, now confident that he would win, made a critical error by letting Trevor reposition himself. Trevor delivered the killing blow. He let his victim fall to the ground where he stood, and moved on. They fought until the Ones started becoming visibly confused in their movements and directions. With the advantage now clearly on their side, his men wasted no time in finishing the job.

Assessing the damage, Visor had sustained some minor injuries, and Quan had taken a small stab wound to the left leg. But the Ones had been wiped out, except for the Ones that fled before the engagement, even though they had outnumbered Trevor and his men by two to one.

Needing supplies, the men headed out toward headquarters. There Trevor would reassess the situation. The men needed rest and fuel.

Three days later, as they were going through the pass, they were met with an ambush. A fierce fight ensued and Trevor was forced to retreat. The Ones had mounted an attack on all fronts. Using their strength in numbers, they had surprised Trevor's force.

By the time Trevor and his men had rallied and retaliated, they sustained two casualties. Carrying their dead and wounded, they stopped at an outpost near the base of the mountains. Handing out water, Trevor spoke to each man in turn, inquiring about their health. Nash, one of Trevor's finest snipers, had taken a hit. His leg appeared to be shattered.

As Trevor approached, Nash spoke, "I'll be alright sir—certainly better than Hans and Kipper."

Trevor pushed away the stinging realization that he had lost two good men. He would deal with this newest blot on his soul at a later date.

Trevor spoke, "Just take care, soldier. I expect you up and ready, in a few days time."

"Yes, sir."

As expected, the Ones were in hot pursuit. They smelled blood and liked it. That was just fine with Trevor. This time, he would have a surprise of his own. It was payback time.

Jacques, the commander of the small force that had attacked Trevor, was confident the supreme leader would be most impressed. Jacques had taken the initiative and had attacked Trevor at the pass.

It would earn him a position of distinction, one he deserved. Fundor would ask him to head one of the southern offices and he would graciously accept. He would rule in just a few years' time. He would finish the job, here and now. They appeared to be vulnerable—just sitting there for the taking. Jacques moved into position. He intended to crush the resistance.

His right hand man stood beside Jacques.

"Sir, if I may say so, the men are uneasy. They think it may be a trick. I would …"

The soldier fell to the ground before he could continue. Choking, gasping for air, he collapsed. No one questioned Jacques' authority. Jacques' cold, empty eyes turned to the soldiers before him. They bowed their heads in compliance.

The man was still alive. Jacques liked torture. The Ones looked up at Jacques as he walked over to him. By the look on the face of the Ones, he knew he was about to die.

"The buzzards need sustenance too." Jacques kicked his limp body down the ravine as he turned and walked away. A few brief screams could be heard.

Jacques' men moved into position. They swooped in and surrounded the group of men before they knew what was happening. The head of the first man was decapitated. Systematically, one by one they killed each man before the men seemingly had time to react.

When the last man had fallen, Jacques moved in from his safe position. Basking in his squad's victory, he failed to hear what the Ones were listening to until it was too late.

Jacques barely had time to look to his left to register the threat before Trevor appeared and swiftly took him out, slicing his neck from ear to ear, before casually moving on. Deep, dark red blood ran in rivets down his neck to pool around his now limp body. The rest of Jacques' men soon followed suit.

With the white noise controlled, Trevor was able to project his men somewhere else. He fooled the Ones into killing his men. The projection of

Trevors' men had been brilliant. Trevor's men were fine, resting comfortably now that the enemy had been wiped out, yet again. They were ready to move on at Trevor's command. There had been only one most unfortunate casualty.

Trevor, Quan, and Visor approached the fallen soldier who had valiantly sacrificed himself. Theo had held the white noise for Trevor so Trevor could hold the projection in place. The strain had been too much. The soldier's lesson had been harsh today.

They would honor him. He would not be forgotten, but immortalized forever in the hearts and minds of his men. They each said a few words to honor his spirit. Theo had studied under Hallston, the teacher. Hallston had taught him the ways of the Ones. Hallston was a paraplegic, his intelligence unsurpassed, his knowledge a gift for Trevor and his men. Hallston would undoubtedly be saddened with the news. Theo had been an up and coming leader. He would be missed.

Trevor was no closer to retrieving Victoria. Desperately needing to rest, holding the projection had exacted a toll. *There is no time for resting; Victoria is still lost to me.*

Having checked on every member of his force, he decided to just lean back for a moment to two.

He would find a way to make it back to Victoria. She was his only hope. His piss poor life had been just that—piss poor.

He had fought in some of the worst places on the planet and seen things better left unseen. There were things the Ones would do to a man, things so horrific that, sometimes, late at night, when he closed his eyes, they would come. The victims that is, and they would demand justice. They always wanted him to exact justice.

Terrible acts had been committed. Some innocent victims had been sacrificed to get to the top operator. It had always been about the mission. Finish the mission. He had lived in the gray area for so long he didn't know what color was anymore. Closing his eyes, all he saw was Victoria. His Victoria.

Later, in the sphere room, he researched all the possibilities. He called on Alec to discuss viable options.

Chapter 20

They had come for her. Relief flooded her senses. No matter what happened, she found consolation in the belief she was no longer alone. She hadn't realized what these last few weeks had cost her. There had been a huge burden of stress looming over her that took flight. She felt lighter and more joyful, no matter the outcome. The total isolation from humanity had changed her in ways she would try to decipher for a lifetime.

She waited patiently. The moment her jailor fell from the blow, Victoria was freed. The hold had been insufferable. Her head acknowledged the pain but she pushed it aside. She now fought to gain ground for the rebellion. All the doors opened upon her command. A mass of bodies wielding weapons descended upon her captors and a bloody fight ensued. Scream after scream indicated loss of life.

She raced to the gate room. Pushing with her mind, she located the room even though she had not been there before. He sat before the window, looking as if he was simply contemplating the weather outside and gauging how heavy a jacket he needed to wear. He slowly turned when she arrived at the table. His eyes emitted a piercing wave of terror. He wore a sneer on his face.

"You are strong, Victoria—stronger than I had anticipated. My expectation that you would be persuaded to join me has not been met. We could have ruled the world together. World leaders would have bent before us. Wealth and riches would have been laid at our feet—humans begging to do our bidding."

"Your dream, not mine," replied Victoria.

He studied Victoria without speaking. He turned back toward the window once again. "I am disappointed with you, Victoria. I will have to find another way to bring you into the fold. When we meet again, Victoria, I will show you how to properly respect your father. You will bow before me and beg for forgiveness. There will be consequences."

She realized he needed her. That was the only thing saving her really. But she didn't fully comprehend what he needed her for. He was holding his cards close and revealing little.

Silence rained; it was deafening. After some time he spoke again. "I believe I will start your lessons now." She moved to her left anticipating an attack, but nothing came.

"Goodbye for now, Victoria." He moved at an incredible speed. In what seemed like only seconds, he was gone. She turned in all directions but he had vanished. She approached the window and saw far below a shadowy figure moving through the cave.

Leaving the gate room, she made her way back to her rescuers. She was tired; she wanted to sleep a thousand years. She walked along the corridors greeting, hugging, and smiling. A cheer erupted as she entered the great hall.

Men and women stood up and clapped hands while cheering and whistling. "Victoria, like no other!" they shouted.

Victoria was humbled. "Please stop, I am no better or stronger, or more important than the rest of you." At this they bowed over. John spoke from the head, "you are more important than you know. Your conviction to our cause alone makes you great in our eyes."

The gathered group parted ways so she could move forward and address the rebellion. On her left were Ophelia, Octavia, and Acanthus, her most trusted mentors and elders, bowing their heads as well. She acknowledged them and addressed the crowd. "I will humbly help lead you to victory my friends. We have won the day." As another round of cheers went up, she knew the fight would be long and difficult. Although they had won the battle, the war would be drawn out, and many would suffer.

"That is right, Victoria. Many will suffer because of you, my dear." Fundor was in her head, speaking to her.

She looked around frantic. The men saw the look of fear. Anxiously, they searched the shadows for possible attack.

"What is it?" questioned John. He looked to Victoria with compassion. "It's over Victoria, he is long gone."

No sooner than he had finished speaking, he started to gag, then choke. He held his throat as if someone had hands around his neck.

Victoria gathered her remaining strength and tried to remove the invisible hands sucking the life out of her friend. She fell to her knees as an unseen assailant slapped her in the face. The slap was incredibly forceful; it threatened to knock her out. She knew he was far away, because his power was beginning to dwindle.

She could do this. She must, for John's eyes started to bulge and he was slowly sinking into unconsciousness. With all her strength, she again tried to pry the unseen hands off his neck; she began prying the unseen fingers one by one. His eyes pleaded with her to hurry, to save him. She tried frantically to remove the hold on him, but the unseen force was too powerful.

The remaining fingers around his throat were crushing his windpipe. A single tear rolled down John's eye as his life force expired. He fell at her feet. His eyes were open, but sightless, looking right at her.

She hit the floor in outrage. John was still looking at her. She slowly lowered her head into her hands wanting to replay the last five minutes over with a different outcome.

"Come, Victoria," someone from behind gathered her shoulders and lifted her gently to her feet. She blindly walked away from the horror. John had been by her side since the very beginning. He had not only taught her the ways of the Ones, he had also readily answered all her questions thoughtfully and thoroughly. He had been her friend. *Why, why, oh why*, she screamed in her mind.

"Because you defied me—my dear."

Stopping abruptly, she shook her head to rid the intruder greater access. "Get out of my head!"

she screamed. She could hear Fundor laughing sadistically. She was providing enjoyment for him. She wanted to find him and kill him for what he did to her friend. Tear him from limb to limb, no better yet, some torture that would take a very long time. Now the laughing increased as he knew exactly what she'd been thinking.

She raced to build up walls in her mind; all the while she could hear his hysterical laughing in the background. When finished, she built a mental door, which she promptly slammed shut. She slumped to the floor holding her head in her palms.

"Victoria, are you okay," questioned Ophelia. Sitting on the floor beside her, she placed her hand against Victoria's face.

"Yes. Yes, I'm fine. Fundor was inside my head."

"This is bad," is all she said.

They quietly continued down the hallway. Feeling relieved that he could no longer hear her thoughts she relaxed a little. This invasion, however, had crossed the line. She felt violated to the extreme. She vowed he would not know the extent to which he had affected her. She would not give him anymore satisfaction.

Much later, when she was sure he was too far away and she had protections in place, she allowed herself to mourn her friend and mentor. John had shown her so many things about her past that she would be forever grateful of. But his loyalty and devotion were not his only attributes. No, he had provided a much needed friendship in a time she had felt lost—at odds with everything she had previously believed in. His gift of listening had been a life saver. Missing him, wanting so badly for him to come knocking on her door one more time, made her feel ashamed and not worthy of his friendship.

The pain was so large, like a hole had been drilled in her heart—so much so that she wasn't sure if it would ever be healed. She vowed his death would not be in vain. She would do this. She would be strong. No more looking back to what had been. That could be no more.

Only now, did she understand the ramifications of her actions. Because of her, her friend had perished. She should have been more attentive to her studies. There should have been more progress by now. Wasting time and energy on her pathetic pity party had cost lives. And, she knew more innocent victims would follow. Victoria would embrace her newfound strength, and she would learn, and she would fight, for all of mankind to have the right to exist and thrive.

Chapter 21

"Victoria does your face still hurt?" Octavia asked her as she moved into the room.

Victoria was distracted by her thoughts. "What? I mean, no, my face is fine but the bruising will take time to heal. I know it looks unbecoming, but I no longer have any pain, really."

"That's good. Victoria, I need to speak with you about the current CVD project. We are worried that the Ones will find out the location and shut the operation down. We want to take steps to ensure our security is untouchable."

Victoria knew of their concerns. She had a path linked to the Ones that they had somehow planted in her. So far, all attempts to discover what exactly had been done to her had been unsuccessful. They had theories, she had theories. She wanted to try an experiment.

She submitted to all the tests known to them. Days had passed since she had insisted they try everything possible. She would be useless to the cause if they couldn't find the path. Nothing had worked thus far. Victoria informed Octavia of her decision.

"No, Victoria—no. Do not ask this of us. We cannot risk losing you. You are too important. "

"I must do this. I have no importance to anyone as long as they know our every move. You know I'm right."

"There must be another way, Victoria. Give us a few more days to unravel this puzzle."

"No, I have made my decision. I will do it with or without your cooperation."

Octavia said nothing. As it was clear she was communicating with someone, Victoria quietly waited. They entered the room and came forth. Ophelia and Acanthus both had concern written on their faces. She moved over to the cot by the window and lay upon the mattress.

As she closed her eyes, Octavia said, "Remember you are surrounded by supporters. Feel our power in you, use our power, Victoria."

She forced her body to relax as she started to chant the words to slow down her life force. As she moved into a trance like state, she saw her mother. She knew instantly it was her mother, even though she had not seen her face for years.

Her mother had a frown upon her face as she pleaded, "You should not be here Victoria, not now. Go back, this is too dangerous!"

Victoria tried to explain but found her words went unspoken. She was drifting farther away when she heard a scream from a distance away. She knew Trevor was searching for her. He cried out her name, again, and again—calling to her, to follow his voice. She focused on his voice. She trusted him to guide her back.

As she tried door after door with no success, she came to a room that echoed Trevor's voice from within. She hesitated even as she tried the door. Something was wrong. She backed away and stood still. Feeling the air around her, she knew evil was here.

She turned and ran to the next hall just as the door opened and the hounds of hell were coming for her. She stopped and forced herself to take control. As a wave of energy pounded her head she quickly blew a blast of energy into the minds of her pursuers. She knew they would not continue into the next path. This path felt sure and true. They could not cross the threshold. The sound of Trevor's voice rang out again, and she knew he would do everything to show her the way.

She now rushed through the paths, joined his voice with her own. She saw the path that led to Fundor's plant. It was a burrow in her brain stem. It was festering into a boil-like substance. She summoned her mother to help her. She called out to those ready to aid her. Several members began to heal her with their touch to her mind and she felt at one with the universe, peaceful and calm.

In limbo, suspended in time, she heard and felt the healing process. There was a kind of soft sizzling sound. There was heat moving its way throughout her mind repairing the damage in its wake. She felt its procession move, steady and strong. So peaceful was the feeling, it crossed her mind to just stay there. There was so much more to do; it was not her time.

She fell awake, back again, upon the cot beside the window. She slowly became aware of the sounds around her, before she opened her eyes to the men and women who loved and supported her. She smiled.

Chapter 22

He was here. After months of wanting and needing, he was here. She had given much to these people—her people. She fought and sacrificed for all she believed was right and true. But she had secretly, shamelessly, wanted this man for herself.

She walked toward him; he had waited so long for her. He wanted her so much so, that it hindered his thinking at times. Sometimes he dreamt that he would whisk her away, far from this place, to a place she would stay safely in his arms. They would make love night and day until they both were exhausted. As he gazed into her eyes, he knew without a doubt, that this woman was all he would ever want, ever need.

She had wanted this moment to be perfect. With well-wishers looking on, she welcomed Trevor and his men. He walked boldly to her side looking upon no one else. They entwined fingers and slowly made their way through the throng of people, to the mezzanine directly behind the row of tables. Within the small respite of privacy, Trevor framed her face with his hands and gently touched her. Then, he kissed her with exquisite care, savoring the taste.

"You are so beautiful. I have dreamed of you each night we have been apart," Trevor confessed.

"As I have of you," she spoke softly. "Sometimes, it was my only sanity."

They stayed there, embracing each other, joyful that they finally were together at last. They held each other like they never wanted to let go, never to be separated for the rest of eternity. That would be just fine with Victoria, but she knew her duty and what needed to be done. Reality always crept in. She would savor each and every moment, grab at happiness at every chance. Nothing would be taken for granted again. Life was short.

She stayed there with him for a long time—needing this. *I need this man; he completes me.* Where had that thought come from? Never, since her childhood, had she ever actually needed someone in the way she now found herself needing Trevor. Was that really what she wanted? Was she falling in love with this man?

Feeling a little off balance, she struck up a conversation. "Were your struggles most difficult? Did your men sustain any losses?"

"Some. I carry the burden with me every day." He looked heavyhearted.

Next time think before you speak. She knew her words had brought sadness to his eyes and wanted to chase it away. "You are here now; you bring happiness to me, Trevor. Look at me."

He brought his head down to Victoria and kissed her lovingly. This felt right. This was the man who would always turn her attention. He filled a void deep inside she had never been aware of. She realized she wanted to see him smile. When he lifted his head, he did just that.

"Ah, Victoria, I need you."

They spent the rest of the evening catching up with everyone. Trevor's men had many stories to tell. In turn, Victoria filled them in on her capture and rescue. They spoke until the early morning hours.

The next day she knocked on Mia's door. Opening the door, Mia smiled.

"Come in Victoria, come in." They hugged and exchanged pleasantries.

"I need your help, Mia."

"You've come to the right place."

Never, since the time of Victoria had she paid any attention to her attire. Comfortable with pockets, that was her wardrobe these days. Needing help desperately, she decided to turn to Mia for help. Mia was a closet fashionista in her spare time. Only too happy to help, Mia enthusiastically forged ahead with a plan to transform Victoria for a night. With Mia's guidance, she purchased a sleek little black dress.

Celebrations took place that night. A feast was laid out for all to enjoy—one night of festivities to come together and share.

She donned a casual yet sexy sleeveless frock that ended just above the knee. Black pumps along with jewelry Mia had let her borrow complimented her outfit. They had pulled her hair up and back in a hairdo with bits of shimmer and dainty ringlets in it.

Mia whistled. "Girl, you are looking good. You will sweep Trevor off his feet."

"Thanks, Mia. You're a true friend," said Victoria. She stood there gazing at herself in the mirror, wondering how Mia had pulled this transformation off. For the first time, in a long time, she was completely happy with the way she looked.

At the celebration, several of her friends remarked that Trevor only had eyes for her. No matter what side of the room they were on, no matter who they were talking to, they were aware of each other and looked over to meet eyes periodically.

Victoria was standing with a group of her friends. The men were avid football fans. Sipping some piping hot coffee that she loved dearly, she commented, "Who do you think will reach the playoffs this year?"

Paul said, "The Cowboys of course."

"No way man. The New England Patriots, my friend," spouted Dion.

"Well since you're talking *football*, I'd say the U.S. will qualify for the World Cup this time round," said Hugo emphatically.

It was good to hear the banter, the camaraderie, amongst her friends. They all needed a respite from the horrors of what they did.

Victoria moved off and let the men have their debate. She found Gloria near the dessert table eyeing the triple-layer raspberry dream cake.

"Hi. It does look good, doesn't it?" commented Victoria as she joined Gloria to stare at the sweet concoction.

"Yes indeed it does," said Gloria. She was practically itching to dig in. Looking back at Victoria she said, "So, how's it going with Trevor?"

"Good. We are getting to know each other outside of the usual fight with the Ones that is."

"Trust me, I understand."

Three more friends walked toward them. "Hey what are you guys talking about?" said Jillian. She was a key Intel gatherer for the organization.

"Men," shouted Gloria.

"Boring," said Jillian.

"Speak for yourself. I personally love the subject," chimed in Cindy. They all laughed. Cindy was currently dating Paul and it was widely suspected she was also dating Lorenzo on the side.

The night was jovial. They each realized the importance of their mission but there needed to be a few moments here and there to balance the stress. Victoria knew only of this one night of celebration; there had been no others.

They all had vigorous training regiments, which included both physical and mental workouts. They each had their own skill set and they handled their jobs with both professionalism and a determination that was unprecedented. There were members of the rebellion from different locales here tonight and there was a lot of catching up on current happenings.

Much later, as the wee morning hours approached, lying in each other's arms, Victoria told Trevor of her travels. "I have learned much, but I need your instruction and guidance. We must go to the Forgotten Caves soon if I hope to truly obtain my full powers."

"I will teach you starting tomorrow, Victoria. We will make plans to move out in a fortnight. Tonight, we have only each other. Tonight, we make memories for a lifetime."

"Yes, oh yes Trevor," is all she had to say.

Chapter 23

They arrived at the Forgotten Caves. The entrance itself was nondescript. Nothing of importance and most notably nothing to indicate a great treasure lay within. With native plants and trees disguising its true nature, the small opening hidden well behind the brush somehow called to her. She could sense the immense power that lay within.

Trevor's men secured the area. "I will be here for you," said Trevor. "Call for me, should you need assistance." With that said he bent down and kissed her lovingly.

"I know. I will return soon and we will explore together." She gave him a brief hug and plunged ahead.

She entered quietly, taking note of the exact path, as she walked forward past turns and forks that lead her toward her goal. She was guided by words from the past. Her mother and grandmother were guiding her, telling Victoria which direction would lead her to the carbon site.

This cache would boost the rebellion. They needed more diamonds for their weapons. They needed more diamonds for their new energy source. Since the lab had been destroyed in Seattle, they had prepared five new labs across the country. Production had already started but they needed this deposit.

Victoria had insisted they use the diamonds. Years ahead of the research, Victoria knew they needed to tap the energy source of these specific diamonds to move the rebellion forward with its plans. The properties in the diamonds here were uniquely different.

She found the site relatively easily. It was, of course, in its rough looking state but Victoria knew this was a sizable find, one that would move all their plans forward in a timely fashion.

The voices started fading away. They left as fast as they had come. Victoria didn't understand why or where the voices had gone. She was to find more truths here. To be sure, the diamonds were a most important aspect of her mission but finding out more about her destiny was the driving force for this risky travel.

Where did her grandmother and mother go? She moved throughout the cave unsure what or where she needed to be to have a vision. She called out to her mother and grandmother with no response. Aimlessly, she walked through the tunnels taking note of her direction hoping that inspiration would strike.

Wandering for more than an hour, she was disappointed. She was tired of this. Perhaps everyone had been wrong. Maybe there was no more to the cave than the diamonds. Thinking her hopes were shattered, she was becoming frustrated, until she happened upon an underground spring.

Something compelled her to sit next to the pool—to stroke her hand in the water. When she did so, the reflections in the pool began to shift. One by one those who came before her rose out of the water to join hands in a circle around her. Her grandmother raised her hand.

The time had arrived for those before her to enlighten her. Looking at the faces of some of her loved ones, she knew some were from a long time ago; she was certain that pure energy flowed around her and there was power enveloping her every pore. They were smiling down at her. Love was plain upon their faces.

Her grandmother spoke. "You will leave this place with power and knowledge. You are to lead our people; unite forces with Trevor. Together you are nearly invincible. Your indomitable spirit will guide you. You are the tipping point Victoria. You must stop the Ones or all will be lost."

Her mother, looking ethereal, spoke up. "Victoria, when you follow the path to this place in your mind, you have the ability to use our powers to enhance your own. Even though we are in another realm, many of our powers cross over for short periods. Only you can use them. Use them wisely."

An elderly man to the left of her mother was dressed in a long, flowing white robe with open-toed sandals. He said, "You are to go to Fundor very soon."

The woman to his right looked regal. Beautiful long flowing hair of auburn that rested just below her hips along with a slim toned body. Her gown was encrusted in jewels that almost touched the ground, and would have except that she had on exquisite silver high heels. Victoria thought she was possibly the most beautiful woman she had ever seen.

The beautiful woman spoke, "Victoria dear, Jonathon is smart and vicious. Be ready for his attack. Silent it will be."

She wanted to question them. There were so many questions she needed to ask. She wanted to talk with her mother, her grandmother. She wanted to find out who these other people were and her connection to them. So many thoughts were racing through her head.

She opened her mouth to speak just as they started to dissipate. She could now see through them and she could almost see the particles of each of them separating and being blown into the next realm. She screamed, "No wait, please, I have so many questions!" But they were drifting away. In the blink of an eye, they were gone.

Being of mind, body, and soul, she recognized her being had forever changed. She felt more powerful, stronger, not just in the sense of body, but her mind was definitely different.

She noticed a tingling sensation, like a gnawing away of the fog her mind previously had been covered with. A fact that, she had never been fully aware of, but now that the fog was being lifted she could see more clearly for the first time. She could think more clearly. Even her spirit was singing joyful music in her head. It felt like having received a PhD without having bothered with the school part.

She left the cave and met up with Trevor. He searched her face.

"Tell me, Victoria. You look beautiful."

"Thank you. I found the cache of diamonds. More importantly, I was told to join forces with you and your men. That I would meet Fundor very soon and …"

When she mentioned Fundor, she noticed he immediately tensed. He was hiding something from her.

Wasting no time she said, "Trevor, I know you're hiding something about Fundor from me. Tell me."

"It is unimportant, Victoria." It was clear Victoria would not accept that explanation by the look she gave him. He owed her the truth. No more omissions or half-truths. He didn't know how much longer he would have her and he wanted to make every moment count.

"A seer has foretold my death at the hands of Fundor."

She sucked in gulps of air needing to feel something, anything, as her world threatened to shut down.

"That will not happen. It will not happen, Trevor." The second time she had said it with a strong conviction. "Who is this seer?"

"My great uncle, Salmun, on my mother's side."

"We will visit this seer when we return. Let us see what gnosis he has."

"As you wish."

The farthest reaches of her mind told her that something was not right about this seer, but she couldn't quite put her finger on it. It would wait. Trevor was not going anywhere without her. This she was sure of.

They moved on to a safer topic. "Jonathon will be attacking as well."

Trevor tried to look unchanged by that statement but she wasn't fooled. Jonathon was more powerful than Fundor, infinitely so. He would be a lethal adversary, one which they would have to immediately prepare for. With her new inner strength she would find a way to prevail. She must and she would; this would be her new mantra moving forward.

Trevor and his men, save for his lookouts, moved through the cave with Victoria in the lead. She took them to the carbon site. Processing of this site would start within the month. This cave would need a team of their best to ensure the safety of the site.

She now understood why there seemed to be so much mayhem taking place. The Ones had politicians in all three parties and had people in positions of power throughout the government and within law enforcement as well.

The Ones hid themselves well and were a well-oiled operation. They methodically moved in circles to instigate and aggravate the masses. They manipulated lawyers, doctors, even veterans, to support their cause. They pitted politicians against one another. They thrived in being the catalysts of global skirmishes.

They were in essence, all that was wholly evil. Their strategy was simple and brilliant. No one was the wiser. Their reach was far and wide.

Chapter 24

Victoria designed a bracelet to her specifications. The diamond, centered, was surrounded by amber gems. The metal was uniquely combined with copper and pewter, the healing properties. She was comforted by that fact. Studying with Trevor had boosted her skills and confidence, so much so, that she knew she could handle Fundor on her own.

In addition, she had the power of her elders waiting in the wings should she need to use it, and, of course, Trevor too. He walked beside her confident in her abilities. Together, they would rid this world of the Ones, be they most powerful and evil. It didn't matter; the rebellion would prevail.

She entered the interior of the mountain feeling his power emanating from within. He presented himself almost immediately. His name was Fundor; but he stuck with the position that he was her rightful father. He was most displeased with her stubborn stance to call him Fundor, and not address him as Father. He stood before them wearing the traditional floor length robe of the Ones. He probed her mind subtly, but was met with instant barriers.

"You have studied well, Victoria. I see you have taken lessons from Trevor." As she did not remark, he continued. "You are now most powerful, but not as powerful as me. Even with Trevor at your side, you are no match for my power. Why have you come here? You have misjudged my compassion in previous encounters, Victoria."

"I think not, Fundor. You have no compassion, no sense of right or wrong; just your overwhelming need to rule the world. To spread your evil ways and take what is not yours to take."

"Your sense of goodness is quite disgusting; pathetic, like your so called friends. Since you did not come here to take your rightful place with me, I will destroy you, and all whom you love. I will rule by a steady hand. These cows will follow me and honor me. They will see me as their god. You will be loathed. I will make sure you live a long life of suffering. Now that you have graciously brought Trevor with you, I may wish to alter my plans for you, my dear."

Victoria leveled her gaze at Fundor. "I have learned much since last we met." She wasted no more time conversing with Fundor. She had come to this place with Fundor's death as her goal.

She used her enhanced power of telepathy and told Trevor she was in position, and then she proceeded to build a false path for Fundor to follow.

A split second is all the warning she received. He looked at her and she knew without a doubt he was coming. Fundor moved with blinding speed. He sliced his throat, killing the Trevor before him with giddiness, then, turning, he looked steadily into Victoria's eyes. Fundor entered her mind through a back door left open. He roared through her mind with dizzying speed leaving oily, slimy, ooze along the way.

Shielded by the path, she lay in wait. His ego would be his undoing. She knew the moment he had taken the bait. Trevor joined her and lent all his powers to aid her. She ramped up her diamond and used it to add to her existing powers. She called on her elders and their power was thrust into Victoria with instant results. The force created a bubble in which he was trapped. Fundor's reaction gave her pause. She expected him to try to retaliate. To strike back, to fight, but he looked to her with renewed respect as he bowed his head. Not wanting to wait another second, she and Trevor cast the bubble to the universe and beyond. He was truly gone.

Thankful that Trevor had portrayed his imagine and held it in place long enough for Fundor to believe the ruse, she felt free to let her stress levels, her fight or flight mode, recede into the background.

Now that the threat was gone, she felt the full impact of how much energy she had expended. Tired and exhausted, Trevor ran to meet her. He effortlessly picked her up and carried her to a more comfortable place; she closed her eyes trusting Trevor to keep her safe. She woke intermittently throughout the day but returned to the healing sleep after briefly speaking with Trevor and eating some dinner at his insistence. They had arrived at base camp but she was too tired to care.

She woke just before dusk feeling fully restored. She found Trevor speaking with his men. They were speaking amongst themselves when they spotted Victoria at the threshold of the door.

Smiling at her, Trevor said, "Come sit and join us, Victoria." Trevor immediately rose as did his men; one of his men vacated his chair next to Trevor and moved farther down the row of chairs. She walked over and sat down next to Trevor. All the men were watching her.

"Trevor has been telling us about your vision in the Forgotten Caves."

She looked across the table at the man who spoke. He had a cane propped up next to him; otherwise, he looked amazingly stout.

Speaking quietly, his men found themselves leaning forward to better hear her. "It has been foretold that we are to combine our forces. In this way, we will be virtually unstoppable. The Ones are growing increasingly more powerful. Our time is running short. We are at a pivotal point—we must stop them soon or all will be lost."

She then spoke directly to the man sitting across from her, "May I ask what injuries you have sustained?"

Nash looked like he might not answer. "Yes ma'am. My leg was injured in one of our last battles. But I'm doing fine enough."

"I didn't mean to pry. Please, do call me Victoria."

"No ma'am, I mean, Victoria. It's alright, you are one of us, ask anything you wish." The soldier sitting beside him elbowed him hitting him in the mid-section.

"Oh, please pardon my rudeness, my name is Nash, ma'am, I mean Victoria."

He received another elbow from the same soldier. Laughter resounded in the room. Their closeness and comfort level with each other was apparent.

When the laughter had died down, Victoria said, "Nash, I inquire because there may be a way for me to aid you in ensuring a more speedy recovery. Please visit me later and I will explore the possibilities with you."

"Thank you. I will."

The men seemed at ease with her. Clearly they were forming camaraderie with her. Trevor was pleased with this development. She was becoming very important to him.

After the men had left to attend to other various tasks, Trevor and Victoria talked together about their strategy moving forward. They would combine forces immediately; collaborate. They each had various strengths in technology. By combining these new cutting edge technologies they would have the upper hand against the Ones. Plans would be implemented as soon as feasibly possible.

Later that evening, while enjoying a glass of wine, Victoria asked Trevor about his past. He had not spoken about his past and Victoria sensed it had been painful. She waited patiently for a response.

He swirled his wine in the glass contemplating his response. "I was a young boy around five or six years of age when my mother was killed. I never knew my father, so my mother's family raised me. I was passed around a lot. I was loved, just not welcome for too long in any one single relative's house. I was rebellious and hard to manage in my teenage years." He took a sip of his wine while looking off into space. Victoria sat quietly giving him plenty of time to continue.

"That's when my aunt told me I was to, 'rise above the nonsense and take my studies more seriously because my destiny was to be important.' I scoffed at her and all my family. They knew nothing about me or so I thought. I was hurting inside and shutting everyone who cared out of my life."

"I grew up hard and fast. Given my lifestyle back then, I'm very fortunate that I made it to adulthood. I ended up in the military and found a home there. Most of my men met me there. We watched each other's back—then and now."

He set his glass down. "When I had served my time and got out I decided to visit my home as a youth. Not more than a week after I went there the Ones acted. I was away for the day visiting some old buddies from school. When I returned, I discovered they had grabbed my cousin, Nick, and had tried to take him with them. Consequently, he was accidentally killed by the Ones as he fought. They killed my aunt as well that day. That is when I discovered the existence of the Ones."

He poured some more wine in his glass and chugged half the glass down. "My uncles told me about them but I was still in disbelief. It was then they chose to tell me about my past—that I was actually one of those monsters. They felt I had brought them to their doors. I was responsible for my family member's deaths and I needed to leave as soon as possible and not return."

She wanted to comfort him, to hold him. She did neither. Waiting for him to continue, she thought how cold, how cruel his family had been. At least her upbringing had been filled with love. She'd had many wonderful memories to help her grow into a young woman; he had had a much harder time.

She would show no pity; he would abhor that from her. In a way really, his entire set of circumstances since birth had molded him into the man he was today. For that she could not be sorry, but grateful.

He continued. "From that day forward I have hated the Ones. As I matured, my men and I formed a tight-knit group. We invested in business and acquired a vast pool of wealth that we have used to help us wipe out as many Ones as we could along the way. Victoria, I don't know any other way of life except killing. I'm not an easy man."

"I know exactly who you are and I like what I see." He held his arms open wide and she quickly moved into his arms.

Trevor and Victoria enjoyed one night of sheer ecstasy. It had been a night filled with each exploring the other with exquisite care and attention. As she lay there in the aftermath, completely content, he began an all-out assault of her senses. Slowly at first, he gently nudged her ear while working his way down her body. It soon became a feverous pitch that she could not stop and didn't want to. He treated her like a goddess giving special attention to everything that pleased her. He demanded to give her the night he needed it to be this way. They lay in each other's arms until the sun rose. It was then that she blissfully drifted off to sleep.

Victoria woke with a smile on her face. They needed to head home today, but she wasn't ready quite yet. She moved closer to Trevor and watched as he slowly became aware of her watching him. She loved him. She wasn't sure how he had crept into all the spaces of her heart, but there it was. She could no longer deny it.

Talk of their future was nonexistent. It was still too unsure. Victoria sensed that Trevor preferred to avoid the subject. She feared he was coming to terms, just as she was struggling to understand her newfound feelings. She wanted to be able to build a life and future with this man. They couldn't wait until there was stability—that might never come. The journey would be sufficient for her but she knew Trevor was holding something of himself back.

Victoria decided it would be interesting to see how long it would take her to convince him otherwise. And, oh, she would relish the time it would take. Asserting herself—being free to express both her sexuality and intellect, was empowering.

These powers, the power of one—one self of body, mind, and soul broke some unseen barrier and sent her soaring with a sense of freedom like she had never known. She ascended to another plane that previously was nonexistent.

Trevor evoked these feelings in her. She glorified in the knowledge, thankful for him and thankful for each person who had interacted with them to bring about their chance meeting. Never having given much contemplation on the subject, it was now obvious that the web of life had led her to this place in time. The people she had been with, or saw, or watched, or listened to, had all played a part. The kind people, the cruel ones as well, had all shaped her life.

Perhaps a person could not thoroughly understand the good without the bad, she surmised. She wasn't sure of cosmic balance, but she knew she didn't ever want to mess with Karma.

Chapter 25

As she approached the home she had come to love, she saw that Mia was signaling for them to stop. Mia had become the closest thing to a sister for Victoria during the past year. She had talked to Victoria for hours when she first arrived—listened to the babblings of a scared and insecure Claire—all without a complaint. Mia had shouldered the burden of fencing with Victoria, running and training with Victoria extensively, putting in long hours. She helped Victoria adjust to her newfound self. Without Mia by her side all those months, Victoria would have been lost.

She sensed the urgency as they came to a halt. Mia communicated that some of the inhabitants in the compound had taken ill. They did not yet know from what source. Blood samples had been drawn and tests were in progress. Several technicians and the research director, Dr. Holmes, were in route from their Atlanta headquarters.

Victoria looked to Trevor and saw comprehension. Jonathon had come calling.

"I want all available data sent to me to analyze. As soon as Director Holmes gets here have him contact Trevor with an update, Mia."

"It will be done. Victoria, Octavia needs to speak with you. She says it is urgent."

"How is she Mia?"

"She has taken her illness with her typical great spirited attitude but Alec and I believe she is not doing well. We are gravely concerned for her."

As they moved toward the compound, Victoria sensed an energy source emanating outward. The elders were doing what they could to protect everyone. But, she could also sense an abnormal presence. Having never detected an abnormal presence before, she nonetheless could decipher that this presence was somehow tainted by the Ones. Moving forward she would now be able to use this information if it ever became necessary again.

"There is no indication what this may be specifically, Mia?" asked Trevor.

"No sir, not at this time. There are twenty-seven people in various stages of illness. Some have minor symptoms and a few have very high fevers. We have quarantined the sick from the well but I fear not knowing how the illness spreads is hindering our efforts."

They approached the compound and saw that no one was about except for the guards. No training was taking place. No one was moving about as was typical for this time of day. It was eerily quiet.

They moved to the front hall and saw cots and a makeshift hospital for the most severe cases. Victoria saw her friends, her family really, hurt and suffering. It infuriated her to see this taking place. *Jonathon will pay for this,* she thought.

Walking down the hall and into a semi-private room, she moved over to where Octavia lay and brought a chair over to her near and dear mentor, elder, and mother figure. Octavia was very wise. She said very little but when she did, she spoke firmly, booking no argument, yet she had a quick smile and a gentle spirit.

"Ah, Victoria, so you have finally come home my dear." She coughed in between words. Struggling to sit up, Victoria was quick to arrange her pillows. She leaned in closer so she wouldn't have to speak up too loudly.

"Octavia, I'm so sorry. I will have every available person working on this. We will find a solution. Just hang in there." This person, wise in her old age, a healer, a respected and worthy person by anyone's standards, was still full of life.

"Listen to me carefully, Victoria. Jonathon has done this. Somehow he has infiltrated our defenses. You must locate his stronghold. It will be near the Truid Mountains." She had to stop because she was winded and weak. Her body was gripped by fever. She shivered uncontrollably.

"Just rest for now. Trevor and I will handle Jonathon."

"No, Victoria, you don't understand. He is only toying with his virus. He is looking for a way to get to you. You must stop him. Should this virus fall into the wrong hands…I need not say more. Know this Victoria, I sense there is still time to stop him, but that time is slipping away."

Jonathon was fixated on finding a way to get to Victoria, and hurting those she loved was icing on the cake. The thought of Jonathon spreading this virus on a global scale was beyond reckoning.

After speaking with the elders it was determined Trevor and Victoria would mount an offensive of their own. Trevor's men along with his whole organization would be available, as well as some key people from the Annapolis home office. The rest would focus on containment, diagnosis, and treatment.

Dr. Oliver, their top in-house physician at the compound, had been working night and day to find answers. He concluded that the nature of the illness threatened to infect more than just the existing patients. Dr. Oliver, a current patient himself, found a mutation in his blood sample that sent up red flags. In addition, he discovered the host range for the virus growing at an exponential rate in a deviated form, something he had never witnessed before. The team that was enroute would take over as he was becoming too ill to proceed. The virus seemed to run its course but came back again within hours, replicating swiftly, which plagued Dr. Oliver. He demanded answers; he was getting closer to those answers through his grit and determination, but it was taking an obvious toll on him physically.

"Dr. Oliver, how are you?" asked Victoria as she walked into the room.

"Just a little under the weather wouldn't you know it. I need to be fully focused on finding answers and this blasted illness is in my way. I need to find answers right away, Victoria. It is a very urgent predicament. I'm fine dear, but I have no time for talk. I must continue my work. I must find answers. I can't help but wonder why the maturation is being manipulated so. Now where is my journal? I know I laid it right here."

He didn't seem to be speaking to Victoria, but speaking to himself really. Victoria politely thanked him and quietly retreated from the lab room. Dr. Oliver didn't really even notice. He was fully engrossed in his own thoughts.

As she made her way down the hallway she told Mia to keep a close eye on Dr. Oliver. As soon as Director Holmes was there, she was to tell Dr. Oliver he was ordered to rest and let Director Holmes take over.

Meanwhile, Trevor had positioned his men away from the compound. They would be ready to go with the first morning light. They needed fresh supplies but it would wait until they got to another base. Trevor and Victoria would spend the night with his men and move out tomorrow. Right now he had to ascertain the damage and make sure security was firmly in place before they left.

Victoria returned to Octavia's room to sit with her. She wanted to reassure herself that Octavia's fever was under control. Octavia had nodded off to sleep. Not wanting to disturb her precious rest, Victoria sat down in between the beds.

She turned to Andrea, who was lying in bed next to Octavia. She had just woken up.

"How are you?"

"I'm doing much better. I think my fever has broken. So good to see you, Victoria."

"As it is to see you."

"I heard Octavia say it was the work of Jonathon. I wish you well in your quest. May the day be yours to win."

"Thank you." Andrea was a good warrior. She had dispatched many Ones to the netherworld. When a partner was needed for a mission, she was the obvious choice.

Waking up, Octavia gave her apologies.

Repositioning her chair, she said, "No need to apologize, Octavia. Your only need is to get well. We need you, you know."

Trevor came into the room and walked over to where she stood. "I will return soon, Victoria." Not caring who saw what, he grabbed Victoria from behind and turned her into his arms, kissing her deeply and ever so softly. He took his time and then released her.

In that instant all thoughts flew out the window. Nothing but nothing mattered in that moment except Trevor. His kiss was like the finest wine, one that should always be savored and prolonged.

Trevor looked at her with an abundance of feeling in his eyes, then abruptly turned on his heel and walked down the hall. *I need a cold shower; no I need to go back to Victoria. I will always need Victoria*, he thought.

It took her a moment or two to recover and float back down to reality. *Geez,* she thought. *Everyone in the room is looking at me.*

"He loves you, you know," said Octavia. Upon seeing the surprised look on Victoria's face she added, "He is not an easy man. Life has been hard for him. He might not yet know it but he loves you and needs you, Victoria. And you love and need him as well." Seeing Victoria speechless, she patted her hand. "Listen to your elder."

After speaking with everyone who had taken ill and conveying the thoughts and prayers that were with them, she left to see about needed supplies. After conferring with the assigned personnel, Victoria felt assured all would be taken care of.

Moving on, she located Acanthus in the main library. She needed some answers to her questions. He was sitting in a comfortable chair with a reader in his hands. Thoroughly engrossed in his story, he didn't hear her approach.

"Acanthus, do I find you well my friend?"

Acanthus answered, "I am well my dear, Victoria, but concerned with current events."

"Do you know what lies in the future? Can you give me guidance?" Acanthus was part seer, part clairvoyant, and a most trusted and wise elder.

"I do not. It has been just out of my reach. Like a veil that cannot be lifted from my eyes. I strongly believe we are at a pivotal point in time. We will rewrite the annals of time."

He took both of Victoria's hands into his own. He looked intently at her. "You must succeed, Victoria, or our world will be changed forever. I am truly disturbed by the unfolding events. Time is running out."

She had never heard Acanthus speak so hauntingly. But she could feel it too. She knew with certainty that they needed to move faster.

Chapter 26

It would take them at least one day, possibly two, to reach their destination. Everyone was working frenetically to assemble all available data on the whereabouts of both Jonathon and the lab. Although the Truid Mountains was their most probable destination, they were awaiting a confirmed sighting.

Trevor had been lost in his own thoughts for most of the day. They had picked up fresh supplies and had moved with expeditiousness toward their temporary base of operations.

Victoria tried to put the pieces of the puzzle together in her mind. There was some piece of information she was misinterpreting. It was eluding her and she needed to figure it out; it was important to their success. She needed to speak with her mother and grandmother. When they stopped, she would attempt to.

The men were tired but determined. At operational headquarters they were assembling their recommendations to be presented to the council.

The council consisted of members of her original organization and members from Trevor's force. Once presented, Trevor and Victoria would make the final determination.

Awaiting their reports, Victoria went to the meditation room to seek advice. Victoria sat on the floor with her legs crossed, palms up. Stilling her mind, drifting slowly to a place of tranquility, she then went on the path to the Forgotten Caves. Within moments, those who came before her filled her being with power and love. She spoke softly, "Mother, grandmother, all those before me, I call upon you, seeking your wisdom and guidance." She chanted it until she felt herself leaving her physical form.

Drifting on a windswept cloud she emerged in a place that was serene. She stood on a dirt path of smooth yellow sand that led to an arched stone bridge. It had recessed lights spaced out across the expanse with hanging baskets of white impatiens cascading down the sides. A slow moving bubbling brook headed down stream, with water that was pristinely crystal clear. She saw her elders gathered before her on the path.

"Please, I need your help. Jonathon has attacked. I seek guidance."

"Victoria, you must go to the source. He will be ready for you. You will have to call upon all elders, living and not, and use your energy sources. All powers that be must be used," said her mother.

A man that wore a long flowing white gown with open-toed sandals spoke. "I am your great, great, grandfather, Theodore, at your service." He bowed graciously. "Never before has there been a threat such as this. Forces are converging at the Truid Mountains. You must make haste for that location."

"Yes, Victoria, make haste," added the woman who wore the jewel encrusted dress. "The walls you have built as protection will not stand up to Jonathon. We will enhance your ability to fortify these walls. Together we will help you keep Jonathon from entering your mind."

"Come with us, Victoria, to the edge of the path. You must wade into the waters. No matter what you see, hear, or touch, you must stay the course and cross to the other side," added Theodore.

She hesitated only for a moment—they were her elders and she would cross. She slowly waded into the water. Instead of being wet, the water passed by and around her and she felt dry and warm. Then a creature of some kind pushed up against her nearly knocking her over. Hairy with scales that looked razor sharp, it turned in the water and passed by her repeatedly trying to push her with its massive head. She had to plant her feet more firmly until the creature gave up and moved off.

Next, children of all ages appeared under the water wailing for her to join them—to take their outstretched hands. All she had to do was take their hands and she could have anything her heart desired. She continued on moving closer to the far side of the brook.

A being that resembled the Ones emerged from the water and offered ultimate power over every being on earth for her soul. He offered eternal life. He walked up to her face and said, "Take this offering and you will have power, everlasting life, wealth, riches beyond your imaginings." She moved around him and he vanished. When she emerged on the other side—her elders appeared before her.

Victoria's mother said, "You have done well, Victoria, my daughter, and so you will be bestowed with powers that will aide you in your conflict with Jonathon."

Her mother smiled at her. She approached slowly and came to stand beside Victoria. She then touched Victoria's cheek with the back of her hand. She briefly ran her fingers ever so softly down her cheek. It felt like a soft feather brushing up against her. Feeling her mother's touch was an unexpected precious gift. She had actually felt the love pass into her being at the moment. The touch was unlike anything she had ever felt in her lifetime and she understood it was heaven touching her.

Tears flowed down her cheeks as she looked at all the great powers standing before her. "I am humbled by your strength, your support, and your love."

Theodore declared, "It will be an arduous mission. There is one among you who may betray you."

Just then from a far distance away she heard her name being called over and over again. Getting louder and more forceful, it demanded she return.

"We are humbled by your strength of character. You honor us all, Victoria," replied her grandmother. "Go, it is time. Trevor is worried about you."

"Wait. Who among my people will think to betray our mission?"

Ignoring her question, her grandmother spoke, "Goodbye, Victoria. May time be on your side."

She found herself closing her eyes, willing her spirit to return to the burden of her physical form. Her physical body weighed her down considerably.

A rather loud, authoritative voice was calling out, hurting her ears. "Victoria. Victoria! Please wake up honey. Please, please wake up," implored Trevor.

"Yes, my love. You called?" She opened her eyes and sat up.

"You scared the hell out of me! What happened to you? Where were you? You sure as hell didn't seem to be here with me, where you belong I might add." Then his tone of voice softened a little. "Are you okay? I can call for the physician."

"I'm fine. I was seeking wisdom from the elders. Trust me, I'm better than fine. They strengthened my ability to keep Jonathon from my mind."

"That's just great. Wonderful." He sat back and said nothing more.

"What's wrong? Don't you want me to have more powers?"

"Sure I do. It's just that you are making plans and decisions without consulting me. It's your call and I guess I don't have the right to demand more." He started to walk away when Victoria took his hand.

"I'm sorry, Trevor. I should have sought your counsel. I will do so in the future. I am in unfamiliar territory here. I've never had to share *my anything* with someone else. I guess I have to learn in baby steps. You are the most important person in my life, don't think otherwise, Trevor."

He studied her for several seconds before he took her arms and placed them on his chest. Looking down into her eyes he said, "I was scared out of my mind thinking that Jonathon had already gotten to you. Promise me you won't do anything like that again without me by your side to protect you."

"I promise."

A knock at the door interrupted what he was about to say. "Who is it?"

"Trevor, I have a communication for you, sir."

Trevor opened the door. His man Nash stood in the doorway.

"Thank you, Nash."

"We have received a message from Director Holmes. He has determined the root cause of this virus is plant based. He's still trying to find the source but it appears that they have mutated a gene. Why they are doing this is still unclear. Director Holmes believes this was just a trial run. He has concluded they are planning something much more profound."

Trevor turned to Victoria. "I have to speak with Director Holmes and look over his findings. Why don't you relax for a while, take a shower. When you're ready, come to the Sphere room and we will go over the reports together."

"Alright—I do need a shower and a change of clothes. I will meet you in thirty minutes. Could you also see about maybe having sandwiches and water for us as well? You must be as hungry as I am."

"Yes, I'm starving."

As he said that his eyes bore into her skin and she could almost feel his lips on her, licking her. At the look of astonishment on her face, he just smiled as he walked away. Had he just really licked her without physically touching her? Could he do that? It was an interesting new possibility that she looked forward to learning all about.

Thirty minutes later, having showered and feeling refreshed, she headed for the Sphere room. She saw Nash speaking with another solider as she approached.

"Hello, ma'am, Miss Victoria," said the soldier.

"Hello, ma'am, I mean, Victoria," said Nash.

"Hello," she said to the soldiers. "Please call me Victoria. Nash you could stop by my room later if you would like. I would be happy to take a look at your leg. Perhaps I can accelerate the healing process."

"Thank you. I will come by later on this evening."

She proceeded on to the Sphere room where she saw Trevor with two other council members, Richards and Gills. Both men had been with Trevor for many years now—seasoned soldiers. All three looked up and rose as she approached the table.

"Welcome, Victoria. Are you feeling better?" questioned Trevor.

Victoria smiled. "Yes. Thank you. How are we doing with the plans?"

"Come, we have much to discuss." Trevor pulled out a chair for her.

She sat down as Trevor put her water and sandwich in front of her. Not being dainty about it, she enthusiastically bit into her sandwich out of hunger.

Gills spoke to the group. "It seems the Ones have reinforced their stronghold just within the last month in the Truid location. Even with Jonathan's cloaking device active we were still able to capture an image of him last Thursday. He is definitely still there," said Gills.

The Ones' technological edge was apparent from their use of holography. They were able to produce highly sophisticated three-dimensional holography at different locations to conceal their whereabouts and comings and goings very effectively from the prospective governments thereof.

Although Trevor's original organization had some of this technology and was now broadening its scope as their forces combined, it still lacked the full capability that the Ones employed.

They had just started going over the logistics of the mission when Victoria felt a stirring in her mind. It came out of nowhere. It pinched and poked at her walls, then slammed up against them. She vaguely remembered saying, "I built those walls because of you." Within mere moments she felt a pressure that was threatening her sanity. She started to sway slightly, unable to focus.

Trevor realized she was no longer paying attention. The extreme pallor of her face alarmed him. Something was wrong. "Victoria? Victoria!"

Just like that the pressure was gone. It caused her to slump against Trevor's shoulder. He held on tight, trying to ascertain her injuries. He had moved into protection mode, ready to fight her demons.

"It's alright, Trevor." Winded, the fogginess was beginning to clear. "Jonathon was searching for a way in."

"Son of a bitch."

Yeah, I know, she thought. "I am too strong for Jonathon to enter now, don't worry. I didn't think he could pull a maneuver like that here. He will not manage it again. I now have a clear marker to follow.

I think we are affecting his decisions—that is a sign of weakness."

As he looked over her carefully, he said, "Yes, that is a good sign." He didn't look all that convinced.

It was decided they would approach from the south side. Trevor would strategically place their forces according to plan. Richards would try to hold the white noise along with another soldier named Stevie. Hallston would be their backup team member.

A second team was assembled that specialized in breaking into secure networks bypassing all firewalls. They called themselves, No Ones. Derailing all the computer systems and uploading an undetectable virus that would fan out to their whole network within seconds was their primary objective. In addition, they were to acquire as much data as possible and recover any hard copies, research material, and anything else that had been produced.

The last team would be with Trevor and Victoria. This team would consist of the best and brightest— the most lethal soldiers of all.

As they had already gone over the plan of assault, she wanted to know what Dr. Holmes had discovered thus far.

"Director Holmes has determined that the virus

is, in fact, plant based as suspected. Jonathon's team of researchers has found a way to manipulate the longevity of the virus and how it can be killed. It was passed through food sources such as rice, corn, barley, and wheat, replicating itself within. He is playing with fire and Dr. Holmes thinks he is testing viruses. He believes he is capable of launching on a much larger scale as well. In addition, he thinks he is trying to narrow his target."

"What do you mean, narrow his target?" questioned Victoria.

"Meaning, he may be looking for a way to get to us."

"Since he has been unsuccessful in recruiting us to his side, he may have decided to either incapacitate us or perhaps kill us—with us gone, he will be able to better manage the rebellion. So is that it?"

"Yes Victoria, I'm afraid so."

"We will get to him first."

That evening, Nash knocked on Victoria's door. When she opened the door, she saw a man standing before her who actually looked shy. *This man is battle hardy—yet shy to accept even a small measure of help*, she thought. Sensing instantly that this man would accomplish great things in his lifetime, she gestured for him to enter.

"Nash, I'm so happy you decided to accept my offer. Come sit down, let's see what can be done."

"Thank you, Victoria."

They sat down in her little alcove that had a few chairs and a beautiful view of the outside. Beyond the bank of windows were rolling hills that were both a mixture of pastured land and natural forest.

Victoria put her hand on Nash's knee. The damage was severe, more severe than he had let on. Knowledge poured into her as she probed for abnormalities. His patella was slightly pushed in and would need a replacement if not repaired. His tibia was crushed, and he had an abnormal angular degree by three centimeters.

She went right to work. Using her knowledge and power, she mentally infused her healing over the vast area encompassing his crus. It was a draining process but she could feel the progress in her mind. When she was done she sat back in her chair sweating and exhausted. It felt amazing—this had brought unspeakable pleasure to her spirit.

"Victoria, are you alright? Do you need to lie down? You look exhausted. I shouldn't have bothered you."

"I'm fine, more than fine—elated. Tell me, how do *you* feel?"

"My leg tingles and I can feel a difference—I think it's much stronger. Thank you, Victoria, I don't know what to say."

"You're welcome. Listen, your leg needs some time to properly heal but your patella and tibia have been repaired to the best of my abilities. You should be feeling much better very soon."

He stood up amazed that he could balance himself without the aid of the chair or cane. Then he grabbed her and bear hugged her so hard she couldn't breathe for a second or two. Trevor walked in at that very moment and took in the situation.

"What specifically is going on here?"

Nash immediately let Victoria go and backed up. "Victoria has graciously sped up the recovery of my leg. I can already feel a huge difference. She actually repaired my leg, man. I can't believe it."

"Did you know you had this ability, Victoria?" asked Trevor.

"No, I thought it might be a possibility but until I tried it on Nash I wasn't sure."

"Thank you, Nash, you have no idea how happy you have made me this day." And before he could react she stepped over to him and gave him her best impression of a bear hug.

Chapter 27

Jonathon moved about the room probing each lab technician's mind, ensuring they all remained loyal. He stopped at Henderson. Henderson's wave lengths were erratic, a sign of instability. He would be an asset.

"Henderson," called Jonathon. "Come here."

Apprehension was etched in his face as he immediately complied. "Yes sir?"

"You have been selected to head my department since the unfortunate demise of Elliott. You will immediately resume his responsibilities. You are dismissed."

There would be no further discussion. No words of praise. No pay hike. Henderson was lucky he hadn't ended up like Elliott. Elliott was the former head of the department overseeing the virus since its infancy. Henderson wasn't positive but he thought that Jonathon had probably detected a slight hesitation on Elliott's part to continue down the obvious path of destruction.

This virus could potentially affect thousands, even millions of people if distributed in the right form. And their team hadn't stopped there; they were now working on turning on a specific gene for Jonathon. The implications were huge. Henderson, however, didn't have a problem with that. He didn't give a damn about anyone else. He was number one in Henderson's book—the rest could go to hell for all he cared. As long as Jonathon recognized his genius and he continued to profit monetarily, he would continue to serve him loyally.

Jonathon moved on to more important issues. The research was coming along nicely. Things were developing slower than he would have liked, but he reminded himself that progress took time. Time, he knew, was in short supply until his confrontation with Victoria and Trevor. He had the ability to see snippets of the future; he knew with certainty that he had to perfect the virus soon if he wanted to finally defeat the rebellion.

The rebellion had plagued his plans for years. And that idiot, Fundor, had performed poorly. He needed Victoria—with her, he could take over the world in short order. He would copulate to produce the desired offspring; his heirs would ensure the continuation of the Ones. He needed Victoria to supply blood for his ailment. Only her blood would do. He had to acquire her unharmed; there was no other option. He slammed his fist through the wall—which gave way to his massive strength as if he were punching through feathers.

His guards stood non-phased. They knew from experience not to flinch. Had they inquired if he needed anything they would have found themselves on the missing forever list. Jonathon's head swiveled so fast that one of the guards blinked and gulped loudly. Jonathon probed the mind of the guard. *No, his mind is stable, no threat. I don't like stable.* He felt the giddiness, the rush of power through his veins. He slowly, enjoyably, expired the life force of his guard. He watched as the guard fell lifeless to the ground. "Remove him from here."

"Yes sir—right away, sir." The guard was clearly shaken.

"Speak no more or you will join him."

The guard moved to remove the body. Out in the corridor, he motioned for the outside guards to enter so that he might remove the body. He dragged the body down the hall while sweat broke out across his face.

They sickened Jonathon, these pathetic people. They were just there to do his bidding. They did exactly as he commanded. They met all his needs or so he thought. He was restless though. Whenever he felt like this he cursed his human side. To relieve the pressure, he always sought a temporary high by killing or torturing.

Torturing was especially satisfying. Not too long ago a homeless woman of about twenty was brought to him. She came kicking and screaming; he had liked that about her. She had been so scared he could actually detect the lines in her aura and see those wavelengths grow as the horrific nature of her situation became clear. He almost hated to end it, but the release he got from the moment of death was so pleasurable he couldn't help himself. Afterwards, he wanted to do it all again—but the bitch was dead before him. They always died, but he wanted them to live just long enough to do it twice—maybe that would prolong his high. They always wanted to die—they gave up the fight too easily for his tastes. The fun all but ended too abruptly. He needed Victoria.

He heard a knock at the door. "Enter."

A guard entered. "Excuse me, sir. The technicians are ready."

"Be gone."

"Yes, sir."

He went into the lab and moved over to the table that had the necessary implements. He sat down in the chair with the arm rest. "You may proceed." He rolled up his sleeve and watched the tech assemble the necessary utensils.

The tech was visibly sweating and his hands were slightly shaking. His first attempt at inserting the needle was a complete failure; before he could even touch his skin, the needle fell to the floor.

"If you prick me, or hurt me in any way, you will pay with your life. Do it correctly, now!"

He had roared the last. The tech seemed to rally—he fortified his will and inserted the needle. As soon as he was done he quickly finished and left the room not wanting to tempt fate.

Although they had found the gene that would be used to bring down Trevor and Victoria, the same gene existed in Jonathon. The breakthrough was almost at hand. This vile of blood was needed to check the progress. His gene would be *turned on*, so that the virus would not be able to affect him. In Trevor and Victoria, the gene would remain dormant and they would have no protection against the virus. He would be able to acquire them easily and the rebellion would be stamped out forever. He would rule the world.

Jonathon had another slight inconvenience. He needed Victoria's blood to enhance his own. Jonathon was one hundred eighty-nine years old and he needed regeneration. Victoria's blood, being the blood of the chosen one, would provide that. Being the chosen one endowed her with special powers she was still unaware of.

Chapter 28

They left under the cloak of darkness and headed southwest. They left for the Truid mountains knowing full well that there would be casualties. The men knew and accepted that fact. Victoria and Trevor were determined to do all they could to prevent that. *She must and she would*, she reminded herself.

It took them two days to safely make their way to the Truid Mountains. Once there, they set up a base of operations close by in a locale that would be unseen from both the Ones and the local authorities.

The onslaught took place just past ten o'clock. She remembered because the morning had started with the wildlife going about its normal routine of everyday survival, unbeknown to the devastation that would soon take place. As they moved forward, however, the animals ran for cover as if sensing the imminent danger.

The wind blew with ferocity. There was a shift in the energy all around them. The air became chilled mere moments before the first wave of Ones soared through the entrance to attack.

Each soldier, man and woman, fought bravely. As Victoria moved through the throngs of bodies, of mayhem, she noticed an Ones using his mind control to bring a soldier to her knees. She had both hands covering her ears—but that would not help. Victoria ignored the others as she used her own form of mind control that brought that Ones looking her way. She silently screamed into his mind at a high pitched frequency. That gave the soldier time to rise and dispatch that Ones to the netherworld. *Good riddance.* She moved on after the soldier nodded her head in thanks.

Trevor was in the midst of two Ones attacking him. The first hit him with a pulse, while the second tried to inject a mind numbing sequence. The Ones closed in as Trevor appeared to be adversely affected. As the Ones rammed into him and knocked him to the ground, he rolled to his right and delivered the first deathblow. However, the second Ones used that time to stab him between the shoulder blades and began to twist the blade.

Victoria felt his pain. As the knife was being twisted she could only shake from the blow. They were now so connected she knew instantly when he felt distress; he couldn't block it. She hurled a burst of stabbing pain so severe that the Ones exploded into pieces of red dust.

Not being in the same room as Trevor, she tried to make her way back to him. There were too many Ones between her and Trevor. More poured into the hall. Several Ones had eyes only for her. Trouble was coming her way.

Where are Richards and Stevie? What about Hallston? Why isn't the white noise being neutralized? she questioned.

Trevor rose and used his knife to kill three more Ones. There seemed to be an endless supply. *Where the hell are Richards and Stevie?* he wondered. They should have had it under control by now.

Several fresh Ones poured into the area. They needed a new plan.

"Quan, are you there?" He spoke telepathically to Quan. Quan always had had the ability since birth. They had discovered each other's abilities during a battle overseas many years ago and had used that to their advantage many times over. Both their lives had been saved because of it and Quan's loyalty to Trevor was unquestionable.

"Yes, I'm here, sir."

"We need to go to Plan Alfa Dog, now."

"Yes, sir."

Quan notified all team leaders that Plan Alfa Dog was to be implemented immediately. Each team leader had been specially fitted with a diamond bracelet that had been designed by Victoria. The new energy source they were still learning about would give them limited powers to hold down the white noise within a short range. It would have to do.

Meanwhile, Victoria was trying to make her way into the outer room when Fundor appeared. He smiled when Victoria gasped.

"Yes my dear, I am very much alive. You did not dispatch me to the universe and beyond as you had wished."

Jonathon appeared as well. "Do not interfere; she is mine, Fundor." Fundor did not reply.

Jonathon looked at her then. He moved swiftly to her side and grabbed a fist full of her hair and yanked her to the right. But Fundor was faster; he hit her with a device that started numbing her legs within seconds. She fell to the ground hard even with Jonathon still holding her by the hair.

"You have interfered for the last time, Fundor," yelled Jonathon. Fundor ignored him as he chanted a spell.

Victoria knew she had to hurry. The pain was gone from her mind as she thrust the white noise away from the crowd of Ones in the room. The Ones looked confused and the fighters were able to better control them. At least she could do this for her friends and family if only for a short time.

Fundor was enraged. As he prepared a new surprise for Victoria, Jonathon thrust Victoria all the way to the ground and grabbed Fundor by the throat. He threw Fundor across the room and partially into the stone wall. Fundor retaliated—he used his mind to pick up Jonathon and attempted to choke him while his feet were dangling several inches off the floor. Jonathon simply lowered himself calmly and looked toward Fundor with malice in his eyes.

"You will pay with your life this time, Fundor. You dare to assault me? I am Jonathon you fool— more powerful than you or anyone else."

"You have been spawned from my loins and you are nothing compared to me," retorted Fundor.

As they measured and tested each other's abilities—she seized the moment and tried to back away. Her legs were totally numb now and she could only drag herself away from the scene using her upper-body strength. She had almost made it out of the room when Fundor started hurling different weapons at Jonathon. One of the devices hit her squarely in the leg with such intensity she had to force herself not to scream. Looking at her leg, as if in slow motion, she saw a slow then much faster flow of her blood spill onto the floor beside her. Within seconds her clothing was wet as blood soaked her clothes. It all seemed surreal.

Jonathon and Fundor fought for several seconds before Fundor fled out of the room with Jonathon in fast pursuit. With them out of the room, it was much easier for the fighters to gain the upper hand. Each fighter was battling at least two Ones. *The odds are not in our favor*, she thought.

She looked to her left and saw Trevor fighting to get to her. She knew he would be too late. She should have told him before now. Not wanting him to be forced into a position to declare his love, she had withheld telling him she loved him. She withheld from telling him that he was her world—that he completed her in all the ways that were important. Now, she lay there full of regret. Now it was too late. He would never know. He would never know.

Calmness overcame her and she felt herself getting cold, but it didn't seem to really bother her. Peacefulness was setting in. Looking up she could see an image of a full moon up in the sky just above the tree tops. It was a comfortable temperature and there were fireflies dancing in the trees. It was still daylight but the transition between day and night had begun. The moon would be beautiful tonight. She heard voices coming from somewhere just beyond the trees. *I wonder who's there. Perhaps I should go and see*, she thought.

An ear splitting scream erupted from Trevor's mind into hers. "No—Victoria—no. I command you—I demand that you hold on—no matter what you hold on. You hear me—you hold on dammit!" Even though things were starting to become fuzzy and cold she could do no other. He wanted her to hold on and so she must. She gathered all her remaining energy and called for the aid of those before her to help her wait for Trevor. She wanted to tell him something important. She held on to that need like never before.

He sliced the jugular without a care of the Ones before him—nothing mattered but getting to Victoria—his Victoria. He screamed silently to the heavens above to please, please help her hold on. He downed one more Ones before he hurled himself to her side, trusting his men to watch his back. She was barely conscious now. He put his hands on her heart and demanded she wake up.

"Listen, Victoria. Hear me honey."

She interrupted whatever he was saying. It was paramount she tell him something but whatever that something was she had forgotten it. A second later it came back to her and she rushed to get it out. "Trevor, know this—remember this—I love you."

He paused long enough to look into her eyes as a tear started to slowly make its way down his cheek. "Victoria, listen to me woman. Use your power of healing aided by my strength to repair the torn artery. You are bleeding out. You can do this. You must do this—-do you hear me?"

He paid no attention to the ensuing fight. Nash and Quan had his back. He needed to put his entire focus into saving Victoria.

She could feel his power flowing into her and she knew she was now stronger. She would try. She called on all of those before her and all her elders. She immediately felt more power surging into her being. She slowly, carefully, so not to cause more damage, started ascertaining the extent of the damage. Once she determined the best way forward, she pieced the artery back together. The muscles and tendons were a mess; it took a surgeon's hand to piece it all back together. It took all the energy she had—all the skill she could muster—with hopefully a small measure of luck thrown in too, for her to cauterize the wound. She vaguely remembered hearing Trevor say he loved her right before she blacked out.

Chapter 29

Waking up with the smell of herbs and roses filling her nostrils, she slowly turned her head and discovered she was in a massive bed with beautiful furnishings within her peripheral vision. Sitting in a chair positioned next to the bed slept Trevor. He had bags under his eyes and his clothes looked slept in. *Why is he sleeping in a chair?* she pondered.

Memories came back in a rush and she realized he had saved her; he was her own personal hero. She wondered if he had really said he loved her or if that was simply a figment of her imagination. She looked lovingly at Trevor. He looked beautiful to her. He was proud, and arrogant at times, kind and brave, and sometimes a royal pain, but she loved him. Oh she loved him alright. Whatever time they had left together she vowed to make the most of each day. Each day was a gift from above and she was eternally grateful to have a second chance.

"Hello beautiful." He moved over to gently take her hand. "I've missed you. How are you feeling?"

"I've had better days but I feel relatively fine. What day is it?"

"Friday, the 14th—you have been here for almost three days now."

"Three days! Wow, what happened? How are the soldiers? Should I try to heal anyone? Perhaps I should get up and go and see about the wounded."

He put a staying hand on her arm. "You, my lady, aren't going anywhere." When she started to speak he gave her a look that said he meant what he said. "You are wounded; you will stay here until you are one hundred percent cleared by the physician, even if I have to tie you down." He had said that last part about the 'tie you down' with a glint in his eyes and smirk on his face. "The soldiers are being tended to by competent staff, Victoria—don't worry about anything but getting well for right now. Tomorrow will come soon enough."

"Alright, Trevor." She had known it would be useless to argue with him so she saved her breathe.

Four days later, the physician, at Victoria's insistence, cleared her to eat with everyone currently in residence. Dr. Nichols also approved a plan for her to take a short excursion outside for some much needed fresh air and sunshine.

After a meal fit for a queen, she realized how much she had missed the interaction with all the people of the rebellion. She looked around the room and saw the faces of friends near and dear to her heart. Sometimes it was a burden having a lack of privacy but they all respected each other's wishes and they were stronger and safer together. She was content.

After their meal, Trevor insisted she rest. The library was her first thought so she made her way there and did some research on the Ones. It was apparent that the Ones had indeed left their home planet that was 13.3 billion light years away because they had committed crimes against their kind so unspeakable that it had warranted their expulsion.

Perhaps the leaders of their kind thought that they would succumb to a hideous death in space. But she thought it had been totally irresponsible to have unleashed such evil without knowing what exactly they would do if they succeeded in escaping death. For all their advancements, perhaps the leaders had not been all that smart after all. She sat there for hours studying all that was known about the Ones. She had studied this material before but rereading it seemed important right now.

Sometime later, Trevor took her beside the lake a short distance from the main house. He laid a blanket down on the soft grass. The kitchen staff had generously packed some wine and cheese, along with some appetizers. It was delicious and filling. The sun was slowly making its way toward sunset and the water shone with different shades and shapes from the weeping willows gently blowing in the breeze.

"It's so peaceful here, Trevor, thank you. This is an unexpected pleasure."

"My pleasure, Victoria."

He had said little since arriving. She sensed he wanted to ask her something but didn't know how to form the question. *This could be bad. Maybe he wants to end things between us but doesn't want to hurt my feelings*, she thought. She decided she shouldn't worry until she knew what he wanted. Instead, she turned and studied the lake, taking in all its beauty, from the little ripples in the water caused by fish and frogs, to the lone crane searching the shallows for dinner.

Finally he said, "The sun is about to go down, perhaps we should pack up now."

They headed back to the room. Victoria didn't want to admit it but she was tired. Not wanting Trevor to know, she pleaded a headache and said she wanted to read a little. He went to check on the plans and said he would return later.

She returned to the library wanting to finish the book she had discovered about the Ones. It contained information she had previously read but there was still more to be read. As she opened the book to her bookmarked page she realized that there weren't any page numbers on these particular pages near the rear of the book. *That's odd, why wouldn't there be any page numbers?*

She read, "13.3 billion light years from Earth, the Ones came as a small group of convicted prisoners near death. On Earth they discovered their powers were superior to the species inhabiting the planet. The Ones quickly set a course to overpower the planet. Their longevity is prolonged by finding the chosen one and using the blood as an enhancer, thus providing many more years to the consumer." Victoria was stunned. She was sure she had never read this page before. The ramifications smacked her in the face like a baseball bat. *My god, imagine the possibilities. No wonder they want to acquire me.*

She closed the book and sat back in her chair. There were apparently many more things she was unaware of concerning the Ones. She opened the book to continue reading. "Finding the right mate is essential for the chosen one, as their offspring is essentially more powerful given the right circumstances, or as powerful as the Ones themselves. There is but one that will change the course of history."

Closing the book, she picked it up and returned it to the shelf. "Trevor, can you meet me in the library please, it is essential I show you a passage in this book."

"Yes, of course. I will be right there."

She rarely talked with Trevor using telepathy. She was new to using it and found it was still a little draining. It would take some training to fully utilize this new mode of communication. It came in quite handy at times.

When Trevor walked into the library she immediately sensed his presence. When he walked into a space, he owned it. Never before having met any person, man, woman, or child, that could accomplish that feat, he was unique and special—and hers. She wanted that to be true.

She pulled the book from the shelf. She flipped through the pages to the back of the book. The page numbering ended on the last page. There were no other unnumbered pages at the rear of the book. Those unnumbered pages were missing.

"It was right here. I found unnumbered pages at the rear of this book and now they're gone."

"What did it say?"

"It said that their life span is prolonged by finding the chosen one and using their blood. It also stated that the chosen one must find the right mate because their offspring could potentially be more powerful than the Ones themselves."

"Damn."

"Then there was the last part that stated, 'there is but one that will change the course of history.'"

Trevor and Victoria talked for a while more contemplating the implications. Trevor finally said, "Victoria, it grows late, we should retire to our rooms. Come."

In bed, Trevor held her but was in deep thought. Victoria too was in deep thought reeling with all the possibilities. They didn't speak—just held each other.

Later that same evening Trevor turned to her in bed and said, "I want to talk to you about a few things."

"Oh, sounds serious."

"It is to me."

That caught her attention. "Then tell me, Trevor, what's on your mind?"

"I have been thinking a lot lately about our relationship."

Victoria wasn't sure she wanted to walk down this particular road. She didn't know where it might lead her. "You don't have to say anything, Trevor, there's no pressure. I am happy just the way we are."

"You don't understand. I want you to know that I love you. I love you in every possible way for a man to love a woman. I am asking you, Victoria, to be my wife."

"Yes."

"Yes?"

"Definitely yes—I love you so very much, Trevor, always and forever. "

No more words were needed for the rest of the night, one filled with exploration, discovery, and ecstasy.

On the other side of the world:

Jonathon was licking his wounds and biding his time. Fundor, the idiot, had ruined his plans for the last time. Fundor would soon be dead. He needed Victoria and he would stop at nothing to retrieve her. Plans were almost in place; the rebellion would be crushed. This time his plans would not fail.

Please enjoy an excerpt from my upcoming book,

A LIFETIME TO WAIT
(THE DARKEST SERIES)

He came out of nowhere, tackling her to the ground like a battering ram, milliseconds before she felt the heat from the beam of light. It had just missed them. Thankfully, he had rolled them to the right. Jerking her up by her shirt, he pulled her along to the edge of the forest. Wedged between him and a large Sycamore tree, she barely had time to look at his face, when the tree was hit with such force a large portion of its top half exploded and came raining down. He took her hand and ran through the forest.

Sprinting farther into the interior, he abruptly turned sharply to his left and ran at break-neck speed for the riverbank. Her heart was pounding; she was finding it difficult to understand the events unfolding before her. Running over tree roots and rocks, the man was unknowing or uncaring that she would falter any second now and they would both go tumbling over the rocky trail. She knew she couldn't keep up this pace.

As if somehow knowing what she was thinking, he stopped for a moment. Out of breath, she leaned over putting both hands on her knees for support. She began contemplating what exactly was going on, when he pulled her forward slowly. She was rudely awakened from her thoughts when the ice cold water hit her senses.

"Here Brooke, take this, hurry."

He handed her a reed. She grabbed the reed and took a life-saving deep breath a mere moment before he shoved her face underwater. He squeezed in close to her and none-too-gently pushed her up against the embankment. The cold was slowly seeping into her pores and making her brain foggy.

She wasn't sure if she was still holding up the reed when he took her hand. She could hear voices calling her name, over and over again. She started to stir when the man beside her held her tightly, shook her just enough to help her focus. She couldn't see anything, but the voices were near. She felt the coiled tension in him.

Minutes or maybe hours went by before he hauled her up and out of the murky water. She lay motionless in the grass, welcoming the sun's rays pouring over her body. She began to shake uncontrollably. He leaned over her, murmured in her ear that she would be alright, that he would take care of her. She sure hoped he was one of the good guys, because she was fading into unconsciousness fast.

She awoke to the smell of herbs and spices all around her. She smelled some other heavenly aroma coming from down the hall. Perhaps her host had cooked a meal. She sat up and slowly looked around. As she looked around, she saw she was in a man's room. It had masculine hues with little pops of color. She suddenly shivered from a breeze upon her shoulders. It was then she looked down, realizing she had on a man's shirt and little else. *Where am I? What's going on here?* The implications were overwhelming. Lying back down for a moment she inhaled her pillow. It smelled manly. She liked it.

"Brooke, if you're hungry, food is on the table," called a man's voice from down the hall.

She did not respond. Truth be told, she was terrified in that moment.

He added, "If you prefer to shower first, your clothes are laid out in the bathroom."

She quickly walked to the bathroom and saw her clothes were clean and fresh towels were draped over a chair. The bathroom itself looked big enough to be the size of some apartments in New York City. The frameless glass door led to a four person sized tiled shower enclosure with eight body jets. Even the toilet was unbelievable. It had a panel on the side of it with multiple selections available. *How many features did a toilet need to have?* she wondered. She locked the door and took a luxurious shower. Using all the body jets, she let the water wash over her. The tension slowly washed away, easing her many aches and pains, and she thoroughly enjoyed herself. She took her time dressing and blow drying her hair. She found a mini hairbrush on the counter and helped herself.

She was afraid to open the door. Who was this man? What was the intent? Who had undressed her? How had she arrived here? And where was here? So many questions, enough stalling. Besides, she needed to eat, as she was beginning to feel light-headed.

She opened the door. In the doorway stood a man that was formidable looking and really, really strong. She had serious thoughts about closing the door and locking it again.

Then, he smiled at her. Her knees threatened to give out. That look could make women swoon. He was leaning against the wall, his arms crossed over his chest. He had short, cropped, baby-fine blond hair, with dark blue eyes. His dark tan told her he mainly stayed outdoors.

"Aren't you hungry, Brooke?" He reminded her of a mythical, Greek god.

"Yes, I am, but I want some answers first."

"Come and sit down. With food in your belly, your mind will focus better."

She couldn't argue with that. She followed him to the kitchen. A long set of windows banked the far wall and highlighted the massive mountains in the foreground. What she saw out the windows was breathtaking. Mountains, some taller than she could see to the tops, others smaller in size, but all of them full of trees, green and lush, was a sight to see. And, she was sure, full of life.

The kitchen itself was impressive with all the latest appliances and gleaming granite countertops. It had a huge island with stools on one side, the six burner gas cooktop on the opposite side. Before her, a feast was laid out. She hopped onto one of the stools and helped herself to a strawberry. Just before she put it in her mouth she challenged, "Aren't you going to join me?"

He laughed. "No. I was so hungry and you were peacefully sleeping, so I helped myself earlier. It's not poison, Brooke. If that had been my intention, you would already be dead."

She shrugged. She had already figured that out for herself and had decided it was safe to eat. She ate her fill and then put her napkin down in her lap smoothing it around in circles. She didn't quite know how to ask it.

"Is there anyone else here?"

"No."

"Who actually took my clothes off? And... washed them?"

"I did Brooke."

She looked up into his eyes. There was heat there.

"Oh," is all she could come up with. She cleared her throat and stood up. She cleaned her plate off. Not knowing what to do next, she returned to the stool.

He said nothing else. His eyes followed her, burned into her skin.

"Um, I suppose I should say thank you. Thank you."

"You're so very welcome, Brooke." He had said the words slow, with heated emphasis.

"How do you know my name? And what is your name by the way? And, where, exactly are we?"

"Slow down Brooke, I will gladly answer all your questions." He looked amused.

She took a deep breath. "Alright then, how do you know my name?"

"I was searching for you. I am a protector."

"Protector of what pray tell?"

"The men who were chasing you, you needed protecting from them didn't you?"

"Well... yes. I guess I did. How did you know I needed protection?"

"I told you already, I am a protector."

This was getting her nowhere fast. He had ruffled her temper. "Listen up, Protector, I want some answers without the runaround, and I want them now."

She had a bad habit of talking before she could fully think about the ramifications. It had plagued her most of her life. She immediately knew she had made a tactical error demanding answers from this man before her. He could break her neck in less than five seconds. Perhaps she should go back to her original brilliant plan. Hide in the bathroom.

He sat motionless and looked at her. "Don't make the mistake of underestimating my sweetness, Brooke. It would bode well not to forget."

She gulped in some air. She slowly got up and backtracked toward the bedroom door. She was getting scared. Hell, she didn't even know his name. For all she knew, he was with the other men, the bad men, all along.

"Brooke, take it easy. I would never hurt you. But I do have my limits and retaliating is my specialty. It would be my pleasure to show you."

He smiled again, dammit. She must have a mild concussion, because she actually had thoughts about what that might imply. She needed to get out of here. She backtracked some more.

He got up. He darted across the room faster than she imagined possible. She was caught in his arms. He forced her to look up into his eyes. His beautiful blue eyes penetrated her carefully built defenses.

"Brooke, listen to me. There's a lot to explain and we have little time before we must leave. I need you to follow my directives for your own safety. All will become clear along the way."

She felt hysterical. She laughed a shaky laugh. He didn't look like he was accustomed to anyone laughing at him.

"Must I prove to you I am in charge here."

She laughed. She didn't mean to, she really didn't. She just couldn't help herself. She must be dreaming. Yes, she told herself. She would wake up any minute now laughing at the ridiculousness of it all.

Then his mouth came crashing down on hers and he took all that she was. He demanded she open her mouth. He pushed his way in, drank like a thirsty man. When she finally softened beneath him, he reluctantly released his hold on her. He gazed into her eyes, and she couldn't have looked away if her life had depended on it.

"Brooke we need to leave soon. Can you please trust me? We will talk further tonight. I promise to make things clear."

He hadn't released her fully. She was still in his embrace.

"What is your name?"

"My name is Dragone."

"Okay, Dragone."

"Okay what?"

"Okay, I will wait until this evening to get all my questions answered. All, Dragone." He released her and she hastily retreated to the bedroom.

He had given her privacy these last 30 minutes. She had a lot on her plate. He would try to make her understand.

"My pack is ready Brooke. It's getting late, are you ready to go?"

There was no response. He moved with speed throughout the house. She was gone. The little minx had tricked him. He was furious. She would pay this time.

A special thanks to my readers. I have dreamed of being an author for many years now. Inspired by writers before me, I took the plunge—but without you, the reader, my dreams would be just that—dreams. ~ Jackie Mae

Please connect with me:

 Like me on Facebook at:
www.facebook.com/AuthorJackieMae

Follow me on Twitter at:
www.twitter.com/@jackiemaeauthor

Contact Information:

Email: jackiemaebooks@gmail.com

Website: www.jackiemae.com

Order my next book in the series:

A LIFETIME TO WAIT
(THE DARKEST SERIES) can be found on Amazon.com. For further information concerning the sale of this book please visit http://www.jackiemae.com.